I0583947

Metaphorosis

December 2020

Beautifully made speculative fiction

Also from Metaphorosis

<u>Verdage</u>

Reading 5X5 x2: Duets
Score – an SFF symphony
Reading 5X5: Readers' Edition
Reading 5X5: Writers' Edition

<u>Metaphorosis Magazine</u>

Metaphorosis: Best of 20xx
Metaphorosis 20xx: The Complete Stories
annual issues, from 2016

Monthly issues

<u>Plant Based Press</u>

Best Vegan Science Fiction & Fantasy
annual issues, from 2016

from B. Morris Allen:
Susurrus
Allenthology: Volume I
Tocsin: and other stories
Start with Stones: collected stories
Metaphorosis: a collection of stories

Metaphorosis

December 2020

edited by
B. Morris Allen

ISSN: 2573-136X (online)
ISBN: 978-1-64076-183-4 (e-book)
ISBN: 978-1-64076-184-1 (paperback)

Metaphorosis
a magazine of speculative fiction
from
Metaphorosis Publishing

Neskowin

December 2020

The Skin of Aquila Cadens

Chris Panatier

TRANSMISSION T+10968.0
Authenticate: M. Saenz, Research Barque *Lyrae*

Pod is down from the *Lyrae*, upright and undamaged. Aquila Cadens, population: one. Surface scans show polymorphs of calcium carbonate with intergrowths of dolomite and huntite, limestone. Visual identification of a large iron deposit near the water to the East. No apparent vegetation. No apparent life, unfortunately, but I have only surveyed megascopically. I will put soil samples under glass tomorrow, hopefully. I'll move on to the water after that. See what swims.

Maricella dispatched the message. It wouldn't reach home for twenty-five years. She'd be eighty-nine by then, having long since completed her mission and quit the planet. She leaned over to flip down a row of switches and caught a glimpse of herself in the pod's display screen. The woman that reflected back had been young when she'd set out from Earth almost eleven thousand days ago. She raised an eyebrow and sighed. Half of her life spent transecting the void.

She sealed her helmet and crawled from the pod to stand on the bleached and crumbling caliche-like surface. Aquila Cadens orbited on the outer edge of Vega's habitable zone, but the star was a big girl and could cook dirt just as well as the Sun over desert. The planet's tilt was to the black, meaning it was something like spring at the landing site. Near the end of the mission, going outside would be impossible with the heat, especially in an environment suit.

Maricella instructed the pod to deploy the habitat, though it was more lab than living quarters—a lab-itat. She scanned the horizon as the structure unfolded. The desolate setting aside, the planet had air, water, and the basic elements needed to build life, all facts she and her team had already gleaned through a few inches of glass from light-years away. But the distance muddied the answer to the larger question. For that, they had to see for themselves. The short scan she'd done on her deceleration burn and orbital period hadn't flagged anything. Now, standing on the surface, she was still strangely hopeful despite the subtrace odds.

The little bugs Maricella and her team had developed were an evolutionary grade of mostly free-living protozoans, genetically engineered to concentrate all of the best adaptive and proliferative characteristics. Designed to survive in a wide range of settings, a thousand varieties had been dispatched to potentially habitable planets in the hope that some might stick and jumpstart ecosystems. The Earth—the place it had become—wasn't going to give humankind the time, the decades upon decades, needed for probes to reach planets light-years distant and then beam back their findings. Out of necessity, they'd eschewed a systematic approach, opting instead to fire a shotgun, as it were.

In the runup to launch, her team had worked tirelessly to develop the tiny animals for their brutal charge. Maricella had been consumed by the task, eschewing relationships, pushing friends and family aside in her dogged effort to develop Earth's first world builders. *There'll be time for all that later*, she'd thought. But then came the opportunity to walk upon one of the planets she'd seeded. The trade was thirty years in transit—a no-brainer. She'd leapt at it. Her team had identified eight candidate planets and then drawn lots to decide who would go where. She had gotten Aquila Cadens, a tan-blue marble of desert and sea. It came with an option at the end of the mission to visit another planet orbiting Altair, a nearby main sequence star similar to the Sun.

Four years after sending the bugs on their way, Maricella had set sail.

The bugs were chiefly mixotrophs, able to derive energy both from the consumption of other organisms and found chemicals, or through the photosynthesis of sunlight. The largest group would perform so-called 'soft' terraforming tasks—soil building, water and air purification, consumption of bacteria or fungal pathogens toxic to human life. A smaller subset included those that would occupy native hosts and modify them.

The decision to dispatch bugs that had the potential to permanently alter life on remote planets hadn't come without its share of infighting. The plan was to find life and appropriate it—to enslave a microbial ecosystem in order to serve the purposes of humankind. At the very least, they would be eliminating the ability of native life to freely evolve. But if they were successful, if they actually created something *new*, it would mean they had eliminated what life *had been*—an outcome some of the scientists went so far as to term 'microgenocide'. They'd bickered at length over the ethical considerations, but at the end of the day, the goal was to save the human race. And if it's us versus them, well...

The whole endeavor was contingent on the panspermia hypothesis of life proliferation being correct—that life in the local area of the galaxy shared a common source. If alien genetics were governed by something other than DNA, their bugs would be impotent to carry out their charge, and any philosophical misgivings would remain academic.

The mission allowed just over one Earth-year for surveys and analysis before she had to be up and away. At that time she'd have a choice: aim for home or Altair. The *Lyrae* was fast, but making either destination was dependent on a lone slingshot opportunity with Vega that came in four hundred days' time. Miss that window and she'd be the first human to die on Aquila Cadens.

With the labitat expanded and filling with atmosphere, she grabbed a collection kit from an outer compartment and headed east to where a range of rippling dunes signaled the sea's boundary.

The distance to the shore—only about a thousand meters—felt double in her suit. She hoped it was more the gravity and heat and less the effects of age. In her head she was still thirty-four. At the foot of a large dune, she stopped to catch her breath and hydrate, then took the ascent deliberately, pacing herself to make it up in one steady go.

From north to south, the sea was red. Maricella coughed out a laugh, felt her eyes tearing at the sight. Ignoring her exhaustion, she strode down the face of the dune, falling onto her rear and sliding to the bottom. She dusted herself off and took account.

From orbit it had looked no different than the iron-rich dirt covering huge swaths of ground back home. But she'd been wrong. It was an algal bloom; a red tide. The result, no doubt, of the modified dinoflagellates they'd sent down years before. She trotted to where the gentle surf softened the ground. The bloom meant that the water was packed with phosphorus and nitrogen. So much so that the protists were overeating. Spread out before her was undeniable proof that Earth-based lifeforms could flourish in alien waters. That alone was groundbreaking; fodder for a hundred peer-reviewed papers.

But the floating burgundy cloud was also something else. A telltale sign that the sea was devoid of other DNA-based lifeforms. The algal protists were endosymbionts, programmed to enter the cells of a host plant or animal, graft on the code Maricella and her colleagues had selected, and replicate with the newly revised genome. All in order to incite species diversification and proliferation. The goal had been to create Earth-like analogs in both flora and fauna, riding on the backs of native species. Evolution fired out of a cannon. The fact their symbionts had coagulated into a giant flotilla of algae meant they'd found no hosts.

Maricella stepped into the water until it came to her knees. Viscous, it resisted her movements, so plentiful had her protists become. She couldn't help but smile. It wasn't just the satisfaction that they'd successfully seeded another planet. Their tiny bugs had survived a journey of twenty-five light-years and were thriving, robust. She felt a mother's pride.

She filled several columns with the fecund water and headed back to the labitat. Buoyed by the discovery of her flourishing creation, she floated over the dune and the scorched white caliche.

All night she analyzed the eukaryotes under the scope. It brought another discovery, that not just one species, but several dozen distinct classifications had survived and adapted to Aquila Cadens' brackish water and cloying air. She spoke her findings aloud just to hear a real human voice, lavishing encouragement and praise upon them as she catalogued, even going so far as to name the various subtypes. Desmarella, Rhoda, Aurelia, Gyro, Dino.

**TRANSMISSION   T+10968.37
Authenticate: M. Saenz, Research Barque *Lyrae***

Happy to report with congratulations to all involved that our little ones are thriving. To date I have counted seventy-nine classifications overall, sixty-one eukaryotes in the local water and eighteen prokaryotes/archaea in ground fissures. No native life identified thus far. All details and data in the upload. I'll be continuing my exploration and analysis moving forward, with periodic check-ins.

Over the coming weeks, Maricella explored tirelessly, consumed by the chance of discovery. Her compulsion, she supposed, wasn't so different from a gold prospector's impulse to keep shoveling.

Each new turn of dirt, like each new sample, brought with it a rush of possibilities, the chance to cry *Eureka!*

Every morning she set out in a different direction, stretching the radius of her known world. To the East, the sea. To the North, South, and West, blanched ground veined with cracks that seemed mantle deep. She took samples at varying intervals and depths, plotting the locations so any patterns might later be sussed. Aquila's giant moon was a constant companion, moving ever so slowly through the sky, following along like a milky eyeball. The pod's drones flew sorties out over hundreds of kilometers without noting anything different from what Maricella had seen on foot. Aside from the life they'd sown, there was nothing.

The bugs, though, had done their jobs. Those meant for the soil, a category of archaic diazotrophs, had propagated at around one meter deep, fixing nitrogenous compounds into ammonia, erecting a tentative microbial ecosystem. The waters teemed, swollen and virile, prepared to build new life upon old. But Aquila Cadens was inviolably barren. The rush of discovery from her first day faded, only to be replaced by tooth-clenching frustration. Repeated findings showed the planet and its new denizens in stasis. A holding pattern. Purgatory, in evolutionary terms.

Halfway through the mission, the days became warmer, which meant less time in the field and more in the labitat. When not conducting new analyses or re-running old samples, Maricella allowed her mind to unfold on how life could explode if given but a nudge. The planet was loaded with the necessary elements: oxygen, carbon, hydrogen, nitrogen, and sulfur. Even a modest population of multicellular natives would have allowed her brood to work wonders. She could accept her lot—that a decades-long endeavor would ultimately be fruitless—that had been part of the risk. But her heart ached for the beings they'd created, set forth on winds of scientific optimism, only to end up languishing on the surface of an otherwise dead planet. So much potential wasted.

With the hot season setting in, she could only bear to be outside the labitat in the early mornings and at starset. One evening, as Vega fell in the East, Maricella suited up and headed to the shore where she paced the water's edge. She sang songs. Lullabies she might have sung to a child, perhaps, but now to an audience of countless members. Her red tide. The children of Aquila Cadens.

This became routine. A way to commune with the living that wasn't a recorded transmission twenty-five years stale. Some evenings she carried her melodies into the sea and drifted among the swimmers, gazing skyward as the stars kindled. Together, they devised their own constellations. Something they could share, unique to them and no one else. The Warbler, Saloon Dragon, Sea Fox, Dalmatian Cat... She spoke to them about her life and how, even knowing the outcome, she would do it all over again.

Back in the labitat, Maricella ad-libbed. She ran off-book experiments in the hope of triggering uplift changes in her dutiful spawn, but their fundamental natures were hardwired. The bugs were piggy backers. Absent something to latch onto, they weren't going to elevate. And that was that.

TRANSMISSION **T+10968.246**
Authenticate: M. Saenz, Research
Barque *Lyrae*

One hundred and fifty-four days remaining and there is nothing more to be done. Findings are archived and uploaded. Everything we needed was here, except for the ladder. I will await sling shot and advise of my decision to return home or carry forward to Altair at that time.

Maricella speaks to the bugs, the different varietals. Sings to them. Feels they will understand if she chooses her words carefully, intones her voice sincerely. Carries them about the labitat so they may enjoy changing views and exposures. Her evening floats drag on for hours, so as to be closer to them for longer. She shares secrets. Confesses to them her regret. Whispers apologies. Arrives back at the labitat, her suit's oxygen supply further into the red each night.

One evening, she spills through the pod's hatch euphoric with hypoxia, gathers up the vials for Desmarella, Dino, and Aurelia. Drunkenly, she sways to a song with no name, no melody, rearranges colonies about the lab, perceives the tumble of glassware. Cuts her finger on a petri dish.

The next day, Maricella wakes. Oxygenated, rested. Notes that sobriety brings no relief from the anxiety of coming separation. Abandonment. She pushes up from the floor. On the lab bench is a small tree, red and glistening.

Her little dribble of blood, full of living things. Already co-opted by Desmarella, who has built a delicate bronchus trunk spiked with tiny bronchiole branches. Alveolar buds would surely be visible were Maricella to place a cutting between glass. Given so little to work with, the bugs flex their potential. *Let us show you*, they say. *Oh, what you could have become*, she answers.

Later, silent, she packs her scopes and labware. Places sample columns and vials into cryo for transport, heart crumbling for those she must leave.

In the days leading up to departure, she prepares the pod, clears dust and debris from intakes. The heat, a combination of seasonal change and proximity to the star, is almost unbearable in the suit. She retreats inside, stinking, sweat pooled in every fold, the fingertips of her gloves.

She brings the reactor on-line. Follows protocols. Checklists and calibrations. T-minus fourteen hours.

Night falls to cool relief. She calms, dresses for her swim. The red tide greets her, a bath of her progeny. It is the last evening—she has not concealed the truth. They understand, hold no grudge. And this makes the idea of leaving them unbearable. She wishes them capable of resentment. Hatred at her desertion. Instead, they speak of understanding. Maricella cries until her eyes run dry.

An oxygen alarm pings. She considers letting it go. Even now, the dune is a formidable obstacle for what air she has left. Dying there with her 'zoa, supported on a bed of their flagellae, their tiny hands...she could think of worse deaths. Still, the mission, the future of humankind. She sits upright on the foot of a shoal, her bottom half submerged. Looks to the dune, imagines the ship on the other side, the void, Altair and the Earth beyond that. It is time.

Dawn comes and Maricella is in the water again, murmuring apologies and lamentations. Her mind replays the ethical debates of decades before. Thoughts drift to the cellular phenomenon of apoptosis, where sick cells, such as those with cancerous changes, undergo programmed death so as not to pass on the mutation. And how tumors result when some cells, for whatever reason, refuse to die. She leaves the water and marches back to the pod.

For the first time in four hundred days, she assumes her seat at the controls, brings up the trajectory display. An image of the planet moves in an arc at the end of Vega's invisible tether and two paths emerge. One to a rock in the habitable zone of Altair, and another, to Earth. The countdown begins in her ears, quietly, like a secret. Less than a minute to go. She does not strap in.

As the seconds expire, she considers the blue veins snaking over the bones at the backs of her hands. *Forty seconds.* Their stark topographical relief reminds her that while her body is sixty-four, she's only really lived for just over thirty. *Twenty-five seconds.* She glances at her helmet, hanging nearby. *Ten seconds. Five seconds*. Some cells refuse to die. *One second.*

The panel lights up. Alarms sound. A switch beckons from beneath its plastic guard. Maricella gazes back to the screen and watches until the display re-renders the *Lyrae's* trajectory, and it swings wide of both Altair and Earth. Dotted lines flash from white to red. Apoptosis.

TRANSMISSION   T+10968.400
Authenticate: M.   Saenz,   Research Barque *Lyrae*

I have chosen not to leave Aquila Cadens in order to pursue a new line of research here. This is my final transmission.

I made you. But I did not give you what you needed to do the thing I designed you to do, my children, my issue. You needed life, and so I give it to you. I give you everything. The future. I give you Aquila Cadens. Make of it what you will.

Maricella selects a panel of her most aggressive endosymbionts and places them into solutions containing her own skin cells, plasma, and cheek swabs. Bulk elements are introduced. Within hours, new structures are visible, stretching and retracting in response to stimuli, respiring. She carries two dishes from the pod, one for the sea, one for the ground.

Mother absorbs into child. She feels the bugs, her sons and daughters, her sexless archaea, drinking in the new information and carrying it into nuclei and organelles. Repurposing. She senses the sharp angle of evolutionary inflection, the moment of speciation, the refraction of static paths, now jagged and ever changing. Nature freed to run wild, each mitosis an exponential leap.

Purple veins crawl like roots through prokaryotic nurseries in caliche crevices. Decided by some combination of eukaryotic programming and terroir, saplings sprout without rain, fleshy pink with thick tufts of autotrophic leaves for capturing Vega's light. All-seeing catkins loll from branches. Elsewhere, bulbs burst skyward with petals that explode in clouds of pastel seed and spore that flow across the planet and take root wherever landed. Maricella, gloves off, reaches down. A threadlike root unspools from a crack and spirals around her fingertip. Communion. She feels the cool depths that the archaea enjoy.

Years pass. Maricella grows old within a failing pod that can no longer clean the air or recycle waste. Outside, she is surrounded by the nascent world her children make. She almost abandoned them once. She would not do it now. She prepares aliquots of Desmarella, Gyro, Dino, Aurelia, Rhoda, and others. Introduces them via nasal mist. Children absorb into mother.

Her body given over, they draft their plans upon her substrate. Endosymbionts take to her cells, slicing in and occupying, editing. They weave and sew filaments of neural tissue into harmony with their primitive structures. Sentience shared, their plans are heard, repeated and circular, aspiring upward. Rung by rung they ascend. Maricella's genome evolves even as she lives. Bound together with her offspring, they become the next thing.

Eureka.

Her mind expands into a network of square kilometers below the planet's surface, aware of all each stripling perceives. Helmetless and fluid, Maricella leaves the pod for good, and is absorbed into the living superstructure that crawls to the horizon. The air, once acrid, is sweet and honeysuckle.

Her children bow and stretch, actualize. They feel pleasure and fulfillment of purpose. She feels it with them. They are a consciousness, the implanted code of primordial lifeforms towering from the human scaffolding upon which they build. A new organism is set on a course of its own making, freelancing within the dictates of the planet's offerings. Maricella's body spills into the network her bugs have created, consumed as raw material; the individual gutters to equilibrium.

The red tide recedes.

See Chris Panatier's story "The Skin of Aquila Cadens" online at Metaphorosis.
If you liked it, leave a comment. Authors love that!
Remember to subscribe to our e-mail updates so you'll know when new stories are posted.

About the story

While I doubt humankind will ever send crewed missions beyond our solar system, I'm intrigued by the fantasy of it. My head is full of all sorts of world-building and terraforming ideas from things I've read. In most of these stories, the terraforming either succeeds or fails, or "succeeds" but with catastrophic consequences. I saw the opportunity to tell my own terraforming story with a different sort of outcome, that also addressed the ethical considerations of the decision to spread the human species in the first place.

A question for the author

Q: How often do you think about writing during the day?

A: Constantly. And it takes one of two forms: either as anxiety that I am not writing and should be, or more constructively, as brainstorming plots and problem solving. I do my best thinking while running or bike riding, and the biggest challenge there is remembering what I'd figured out on my jaunt long enough to write it down when I get home.

About the author

Chris lives in Dallas, Texas, with his wife, daughter, a herd of dogs, and possibly one goat. He does album art for metal bands and writes short fiction. His debut novel, *The Phlebotomist*, comes out on September 8, 2020, from Angry Robot Books. As a civil trial lawyer, he represents people who have been poisoned by negligent corporations.

www.chrispanatier.com, @chrisjpanatier

The Three Thousand

Elise Kim

The walls of the city shuddered under cannon fire and smoldered with flames. Its defenders, too weary to march, stumbled through the streets to barricade the crumbling gates. In a dark cellar, the weight of their footsteps sent soft rains of dust cascading down on the faces of a young man and woman who sat huddled there. Somewhere in the cellar was a candle whose wick had drowned in wax a long time ago.

It was in the ringing silence left in the wake of a cannon blast, when the city shivered and held its breath, that she told him, "I believe it now—the three thousand years."

The three thousand years? He had heard the folktale all his life, heard the bards spin stories of the long, slow turn of the wheel of rebirth. Believing it had always seemed to him like an act of desperation: it was the story beggars told themselves to pretend that someday they'd be reborn as kings. But now, at the last moment, his heart began to change. Three thousand years...he could wait longer than that to see her again.

Sound ebbed back into the city. Soldiers barked orders. The cellar shook as a dozen boys who had been convinced to die on the walls like men ran overhead. Waiting in the cellar, they had become numb to this, and the only things real to them now were the sound of their voices hovering in the dark and the awareness of their hands, sweaty and cold, intertwined in a grip tight enough to defy death. The enemy would take the city, post their ash-black flags to flutter in the howling wind, storm the houses and the halls and the cellars, and kill them both—but they would not let go.

She leaned her head against his in the dark and said, "I had a dream last night… three thousand years long."

"Then tell me what you saw," he said. It was a folktale for desperate people, and he had become desperate.

So she began to tell her dream to him, and in her voice he forgot the suffocating night of the cellar, the sharp pain of his wounded leg, the cries of the city as it died. They had been through a moment like this once before, he remembered, in the early years of the siege. Whispering to each other in the dark, she had told him of the places she had wandered in sleep, soaring citadels of glass and beasts that glided like shadows beneath the surface of frozen lakes. They were only dreams, yet when she told them, he had felt that if he waited enough lifetimes he might see them with his own eyes. So he listened to her now, and the dream of their future spread out before him like reality.

"After this life we're born as songbirds, but you live in a forest an ocean apart from mine. Every day you fly as far as you can from the tree in which you slept, driven to search, although you do not know for what. You might have known it if you'd seen it, but you don't: you never reach the shore. Far away, I nest in the hollow of a dead oak and stay there as winters come and go. Each day at dusk, the both of us whistle to the winds, but the winds are too weak to reach across the waters. We die on the same day after three years."

"That's all?"

"We have two thousand and nine hundred ninety-seven more to go. We're born as foxes next. You grow lean, your bones a hard frame for your skin, because the hunt almost always escapes you and you wander alone in the mud and snow. We live in the same wood, but it is vast and winter never leaves it. A hundred miles away, I grow gray and blind before I ever become old, and after five years I lay down for the last sleep. The tip of my tail touches a twig that you broke eight months ago, while you were wandering with a hunger and a yearning that food couldn't feed."

"In your dream," he asked, "do we meet again?"

"Almost," she said. "We go two hundred years without passing each other, until we are reborn as silver fish. One day you find a stray current and let it take you to shallow waters. You see a gray gleam not too far away. Just when you might have come close enough to see what that gleam was—just when you might have seen me, waiting among the bright reefs—a fisherman's harpoon comes for you and the water tastes of blood."

She fell silent, but he didn't know what she was thinking.

Her fingers felt cold, and so he wrapped her hand with both of his own to warm them. "Go on," he said.

"We live and die and live again for centuries and centuries. Once we are swans, and you are traveling through a land you think is empty when you fly across a lake echoing with ripples. You go on, knowing you can't stop searching. You do not realize that I have just landed by the shore. I do not realize that the fleeting shadow passing over the reeds is you. Then we are leviathans, for a time, and we spend decades drifting through the deeps of the ocean. In a black trench where no light comes, I wait and wait. Once you come down, and we glide past each other and our sightless heads nearly touch, but it is dark as black ink and we are only faint shadows to each other."

Her voice was almost too soft to hear as the walls of the city finally thundered to the ground, and the trumpets of the enemy called out, clear and cold. Heavy drumbeats pulsed through the air, announcing with a steady trembling that the city was at its end. This much had become clear to him: the lives they were to have after followed the pattern of the life they lived now.

He remembered how they had met by chance in the early days of the siege, years ago. He had gone with his brother to fight on the plains outside the city walls, and seen him fall to his knees with a black arrow in his heart. He had carried his brother home on his shoulders; then, when he had cremated him, carried him to the temple in his arms. It was in that hour that he had met her, the daughter of a priest. Something had made her sit on the steps outside the temple that day, and something had made a sparrow perch on the branch above her head and cry its bitter and sweet song, and they met with the sudden sense that she had been waiting for him, and he had been searching for her. For a brief moment, all had felt justified.

But the shadow of the siege had hung over them all this time, and every one of their memories from the first to the last had a red tint. Soon the city would be destroyed, and the world would justify what he had come to believe in his most fatalistic moments, that being happy was other peoples' duty, and his was to lie forgotten in the dust. That she would lie there with him only made it worse.

He didn't know how she could tell him these lifetimes slowly, patiently, as if the knowledge of them didn't hurt her. But she had always been like that. In the long-ago red dusk when they had whispered their dreams, she had smiled at the remembrance of the things she'd imagined and told him she wanted to see the wide world when she grew older. Yet in the next moment she said she knew that in this lifetime she would not grow old. Her smile had dimmed slightly then, but it had not disappeared. "We'll have to wait", she'd said, "just for a small while." Sometimes he thought she knew the way and winding of eternity itself. Time couldn't frighten her. But it frightened him.

Shouts and screams echoed down the street as the enemy marched through the fallen city.

"Tell me of the end," he said. "Tell me... after three thousand years, do we..."

"After three thousand, we are finally born as humans again," she said. In her voice he thought he could hear her smiling softly. His heart rose. "You are the son of a soldier, and when you come of age you wear his armor to war. I am the daughter of a farmer, and when she dies, I till the fields she left behind. One day you hear your captain say that there is a field of roses in the valley nearby. I hear news that an army is camped in the mountains above. When you try to fall asleep that night, you find you can't. You feel that you must do something, but you do not know what it is. I sit by my fireplace and sense that I am living in a moment that will not come again."

"And then?" he asked.

The door slammed open on the floor above.

"Tell me. I come down from the mountains, don't I? I meet you in the field —I must."

Their hands were twisted together so tightly they could feel each other's heartbeat, fast and insistent, against their palms.

"You fall asleep," she whispered, "and so do I. When I wake up in the morning, the coals in the fireplace have become cold ash, and you have already marched away."

"That can't be."

"Don't cry."

"But you are."

"I know," she said. "But there will be another three thousand years for us."

Footsteps drummed overhead. Doors slammed open. Hoarse voices shouted.

In the darkness he tried to hold on to the memory of her face, the way she'd been on the steps of the temple, in the moment time had been kind to them. He imagined that moment coming again. "Another three thousand...and then we must be done with waiting. We must find each other."

"No," she whispered. "There will be another three thousand. And another after that, and another and another until the world grows old. But we will come closer and closer each time—"

A blaze of light blinded them as an enemy soldier kicked open the cellar door.

"So you must wait for me—wait for the years to fly past us, wait for us to wander through an unfathomable number of almosts, wait for a time where you and I —"

One day, in two separate forests an ocean apart, two songbirds began to whistle to the wind.

See Elise Kim's story "The Three Thousand"
online at Metaphorosis.
If you liked it, leave a comment. Authors love
that!
Remember to subscribe to our e-mail updates so
you'll know when new stories are posted.

About the story

I was reading Herodotus' *Histories* one summer when I found the initial inspiration for "The Three Thousand". Herodotus is a great author to consult for ideas. I like to imagine him as an intrepid but easily distracted explorer, more focused on what would make a good story than what is actually factual history. He writes this of the religious beliefs of the ancient Egyptians: "[they are] the first who reported the doctrine that the soul of man is immortal, and that when the body dies, the soul enters into another creature which chances then to be coming to the birth, and when it has gone the round of all the creatures of land and sea and of the air, it enters again into a human body as it comes to the birth, and that it makes this round in a period of three thousand years." I'm skeptical if this is factually true, considering how many of his other historical details aren't, but I think it's a fascinating foundation for a story. For several months the idea floated around in my head, gradually taking shape as a myth-like tale of two humans who wait for eternity to meet each other again, coming closer, then farther, but never quite meeting, as three thousand years come and go and come again. Over a year later, the story finally took shape as "The Three Thousand".

A question for the author

Q: Have you ever wondered whether ideas are thought waves directed at you by an AI supercomputer located in the distant future?

A: I can't say that I have, although I know I'll be thinking about it at random moments for some time in the future. It's entirely plausible, considering our rate of technological progress, but I don't think it's likely. The ideas that lead to the stories I like to write, and the ideas that lie at the heart of the stories of the writers I admire most, likely aren't of interest to AI in the distant future. To me, much of what lies at the core of a good idea is emotional, and I have always seen AI as distinctly logical. I have a hard time believing that artificial intelligence can be programmed to think of ideas evoking wonder, emotional connection, and empathy in the same way a real human being living in this age and this moment can.

About the author

Elise lives in San Diego, California, where she spends most of her time ignoring the perfect weather to scribble down stories indoors. When she's not writing, she likes to cultivate her ever-growing collection of fancy wood-case pencils, mechanical typewriters, and crumbly old books.

Heritage

Andrei Pechalin

I used to think my mother had me by accident. Could anyone blame me? My earliest memory is her hunched over a desk, one hand raised to silence me, the other scribbling furiously; her head never once turned towards me. All the while, I shook with violent, wailing sobs, bruised after a bad fall. She left me there for Dad's healing embrace, his calming parental touch, to scoop me up, carry me away, so she could continue her work in peace. It was a template for most of our relationship, until the final days, until she disappeared.

Back then, when I was still little more than muddy palms and scratched knees, my only understanding of her work came from her rare descriptions and my imagination. The slightest change of pressure in the air, a feeling of unease, of something tugging, drawing, stretching, and a small black square would appear. For a moment, it would hang a few feet above ground, like a displaced window or doorway, but without any sense of volume or depth, a two-dimensional plane. It would be completely still, as if surveying its surroundings, then all of a sudden expand in four directions at once, grow with symmetrical precision, like someone was wedging it open and applying steady, even pressure. Sometimes it would grow no larger than a few spans, sometimes it would occlude the horizon, large enough to fit the tallest of the city buildings, but always it would leave an impression of absence—not merely of superimposing itself over familiar surroundings, but disappearing them altogether. They would be back when the square eventually shrank and disappeared, but for the time of its manifestation, looked at head on, it felt like these things were cut out from the world, temporarily transported elsewhere.

When I was six, they decided to call this the Shiftspace. Mum was a member of the first expedition inside. I remember the hours before she left. She was wrapped in furs, a rifle on her back and an axe hanging from her belt. She looked like she was heading into the polar regions, but the truth was that no one knew what to expect from the expedition. She remarked darkly that once they did learn something, this information would be immediately sold or classified. My father laughed and called her a collectivist —he knew that she carried the label with pride—but they were more tense than they dared admit. At six years old it did not occur to me that Mum might not return.

She did return, four weeks later, but she was changed. There were the superficial differences: she was away from home most of the time, at government committees, academic conferences, industrialists' evenings; and she was in the press seemingly every day—first as a hero who had led the rest of the expedition out of the Shiftspace when they became lost in its featureless, abysmal darkness; later as a veteran of

Shiftscience, carrying her authority with a measured, erudite calm.

But something had also changed at the core of her, some tiny, barely perceptible thing that sent out ripples of disturbance, billowing every so often into waves of rage or hysteria, getting worse as the years passed. I would hear her locked in her study, crying, laughing, or screaming, clawing at the walls like a caged animal. And between, I would catch her brooding over notes from the expedition. She would run a hand over her arm, absently, but squeezing and pinching so hard it left marks, as if her skin were a glove that needed to be pulled back over the muscle. There was something so utterly inhuman about this motion, so wrong, that I would run to find Dad and climb into his lap, terrified and quivering. He would stroke my hair and whisper for me not to worry, that Mum was just under pressure from her newfound responsibilities.

Eventually Dad gave up trying to pretend that things were fine. I could not blame him; if anything, I was surprised he had managed to keep it going as long as he had. I saw Mum less than ever, and Dad grew tired of making up excuses for her absences. Ten years spent living in the shadow of her growing catalogue of achievements had fractured his life; stunted his own modest attempts at a career as a publicist; made him feel small, insignificant, a sideshow to her success. He turned bitter and resentful, paced the house with a kind of deliberate, withering cynicism. It became increasingly difficult to be around him. Mum stopped returning home altogether, and several months later I moved out as well.

I applied to study Shiftscience at the Free Institute of Arwall. What other choice could I make? By this time the idea of the Shiftspace was an engraving worked into my bone and sinew.

I was sixteen years old and the youngest student at the Institute. They had accepted me largely on the strength of Mum's reputation. My supervisor had been a member of her expedition, and made it very clear that he could not refuse her daughter. It did not endear me to the rest of the student body or the Faculty, and I kept largely to myself and my studies in a private dormitory at the top of one of the old Institute buildings. The view made up for it: on a clear day I could see Arwall in all its fetid, fuming splendour, stretching into the distance in a haze of smoke punctured by sooty chimneys.

I did not see Mum; I never received or sent letters or telegrams, and she no longer gave lectures at the Institute, confined to a laboratory she had outfitted in Morton, near the original entry point into the Shiftspace. But her presence was everywhere.   Textbook   citations, heliotypes,   countless   theories,   laws, experiments—all carried her name. She had   never   spoken   to   me   about   the expedition, so it was a shock to find her findings   discussed   so   actively   here— supported, refuted, refined, expanded.

I learned the foundational principles of Shiftscience quickly, eager to discover what had kept Mum so often away from home.

The   Shiftspace   manifests   in   places where the boundary with our space is already thin—not an observable fact, but assumed because it always appears in the same half a dozen locations. It closes within a few minutes if no one enters it, but it remains open while someone is inside. There it begins as a formless black void, stretching on indefinitely without any sense of direction or limit. Over time it adopts some properties that are familiar to us. At first it is rapidly filled with breathable air and begins to exhibit something like gravitational pull, though it is impossible to determine its source. Much later, the Shiftspace starts to spawn a fog-like geometry—faintly visible, ghostly surfaces that hint at the partial outline of a tree, or a house, or simple furniture, and grow more defined and solid as time inside passes. It is possible to float amongst all this by exerting the barest effort, pushing through the air in any direction like a caricature swimmer. This ease of motion with little reference point is terrifying; one can become disoriented, thrown off-course as easily as a raft in open water. Mum's expedition had almost lost four people in this way the first time they had made camp, and the ten of them had then lashed themselves together and to their equipment to avoid getting separated.

The geography of the Shiftspace does not correspond to known geography. Mum's expedition had entered it near Morton; they were found four weeks later in Chaing, a journey that would have taken twice as long by the Trans-Imperial

Express. Dad may have laughed at Mum's cynicism, but the possibility of commercialising the Shiftspace for travel was suggested and widely discussed almost the day after the expedition returned.

Mum's explanation for all this—a theory that remains Shiftscience orthodoxy to this day—began by asking why such a profoundly alien space should come to have features that are familiar to us. Her answer was that the Shiftspace wants to put us at ease by mimicking our ordinary habitat. The longer we remain in the Shiftspace, the longer it can maintain the entry to our space open, and thereby better learn to copy its properties; in turn, the less likely we are to want to leave. All of this implies that the Shiftspace in some sense wants to maintain the entry from our reality open indefinitely. Mum posited that it is somehow sustained by our presence within it, so it has a natural urge to keep the entry open, to attract new visitors.

I learned most of this in lectures, and it wasn't long before I began formulating my own theories. I read from a yellowing, largely forgotten first hardcopy report tucked far into the recesses of the

Institute library that one of the members of Mum's expedition had been from Chaing and carried pictures of his hometown. At camp he would pass these around and tell the others stories from his childhood—a way to hold onto fraying sanity as their time in the void dragged on and they seemed no closer to finding an exit. Mum claimed that eventually the images of Chaing were so firm in her mind that she fancied she could see the town even when she wasn't thinking about it. Not long after, she noticed a point of bright white light amongst the darkness. She made towards it and found their exit.

Even though the report had been dismissed as mere correlation, I had the intuition that there was a causal relationship here: Mum had managed to create an exit from the Shiftspace into Chaing by imagining and holding it firmly in her mind. I formed a hypothesis: that it was possible to establish a permanent thoroughfare through the Shiftspace by having someone inside it focusing on an exit point. By extension, I supposed it was possible to establish multiple thoroughfares using multiple individuals. Combined with what we already knew about the geographical properties of the

Shiftspace, a secondary hypothesis: that it was possible to establish permanent shortcuts between different locations in our space-time via the Shiftspace. Indeed, since it took some time for Mum to become familiar with Chaing through her colleague's stories, I supposed that the four-week shortcut between Morton and Chaing could be reduced even further.

I presented this to Professor Jacob Lukash, my supervisor. Even now I remember how he frowned, deep lines cutting into his face with a mixture of hesitation and unease. He looked up at me over the edge of the short essay I had handed to him.

"I understand where you are coming from with this, I really do," he said, "It's interesting, potentially ground-breaking. But we won't be able to get funding for it."

"Why not?" I was twenty, naïve in the ways of research politics.

He smiled. It wasn't patronising, more a pained twitch at something that he did not enjoy explaining.

"I'll tell you something that I would ask you do not repeat outside this room."

He leaned forward in his armchair and fixed me with a hard look. I nodded.

"Shiftscience is of great interest to the Empire; it has been ever since your mother's first expedition. *Our* expedition," he corrected himself with a wince. "The state has been considering military applications for the Shiftspace for a decade: behind-enemy-lines reconnaissance and insertion, guerrilla warfare, that sort of thing. In all this time, your mother has worked very hard to keep the state an arm's length away from Shiftscience—to preserve our academic freedom. She has provided just enough information in some circles, just enough disinformation in others. It's like walking the edge of a knife: make one wrong move and you do not just fall, you are cut to pieces. I do not envy her position."

I remember he paused then and something flickered across his face that may have been 'you remind me too much of her', or maybe just another one of his regretful smiles.

"What this means," he sighed, "is that your mother is *de facto* entirely in control of funding decisions for Shiftscience. And she will not recommend this for funding. If you happen to prove it, to publish it, you risk bringing about total government control over our field."

The following morning I packed a small suitcase and took the first train to Morton. I had not seen Mum for nearly five years, and as the train counted the miles under the steady chug-chug of its wheels, I realised that I was increasingly nervous, frightened almost, as if I were heading for an audition.

I was distracted by a man and a woman opposite me. Their daughter used the wooden slats of the row of train seats like a ladder to climb towards the emergency break lever. The woman grabbed her around the waist just before she was able to reach it, and she squealed with delight as she was first piloted towards the man and then tickled by both parents until she was exhausted.

I watched them, and perhaps for the first time I considered that my relationship with Mum had never had this familial warmth or simplicity. When I was a child, she had spent most of the time locked in her study, too consumed by her work to pay me much attention; when I was a teenager she was too famous to be at home; by the time I was a young woman she had disappeared altogether. And in spite of all this, my father's and my lives had been defined by her. She was not my role model—I don't remember ever looking up to her—but the shadow she cast was inescapably long.

Watching the young family in front of me, a quiet, simmering anger slowly took the place of my anxiety. I counted the years of our family to the rhythm of the train and found that most of them had been without Mum. She was not neglectful; neglect requires a failing of character—some malady or incompetence or evil to override reason. She was simply completely and utterly indifferent.

I arrived in Morton by late afternoon. Mum's house was a detached stone cottage on the outskirts of the town. It was large, but the living quarters were modest, most of the space occupied by a laboratory filled with measuring equipment and calculation engines. The first entry point into the Shiftspace, the one that Mum had used fifteen years earlier, was on the cottage grounds and she monitored it and processed new findings in the laboratory.

She was waiting for me as I stepped out of the motorised carriage I had taken from the train station. She must have heard the whir of the engine or the rustle of the wheels against the cobbled road. As I walked towards the door, raising my collar against the bracing cold, some of the fight I had built up on the train left me. Mum was always calm, even, just short of haughty, and this gave her a presence that far outweighed her slight build and modest height. It tugged me back into her orbit as steadily as if I were a small, barely observable satellite.

I slowed my pace and took a long look at her. Her hair had turned a brilliant white and she had let it grow long and tied it back into a tight ponytail. Her face was a little more lined than I remembered, the bags under her eyes heavier, but she had the same brilliant green gaze. She wore her usual long black skirt and a tightly fitting jacket, all in black, that pulled her back straight. When I was at school, before I really understood Mum's work, I imagined that she must be a headmistress, stern and upright.

She watched me without outward emotion, save for a small, tightly controlled smile.

"Jacob telegraphed," she said drily and let the words hang.

Mum was letting me know that she had been informed why I was here, that she was willing to discuss it, but had had time to consider it and her mind was largely, if not entirely, made up.

The first words she had said to me in five years and they were a carefully judged, timed, weighed attack. She greeted me like a junior colleague, subordinate to her control of Shiftscience, rather than like her daughter. I felt the anger from the train resurface. I made a point of not replying. She raised an eyebrow; her lips twitched.

"Come inside."

The cottage was clean, meticulously organised, utilitarian: sparse furniture, plain walls and carpet, nothing in the way of decoration. There were occasional piles of books on the floor, overspill from wall-length, ceiling-high shelves, but even these piles were carefully organised by subject and alphabet.

"I've brought my work," I said, reaching inside my coat for the notes that explained my hypotheses about the Shiftspace.

Mum reached out for them without turning around, skimmed them as we walked the length of the cottage and entered her study, a large room with a single desk, chair, lamp, and books along each wall. She sat down, leaving me standing. I could not say if it was another power play or she was too engrossed in her reading.

She reached inside a drawer, rummaged through it for a moment, pulled out several sheets of creased, yellowing paper held together with a paper clip and pushed them towards me across the desk.

"Read it," she nodded towards the bundle.

I picked it up, scanned the title: "How to Use the Shiftspace to Bridge Locations". I shot Mum an incredulous look; she watched me carefully.

"This paper," I found that I was reading the paper abstract out loud, my voice growing heavy with emotion, "reports experimental data that tests two hypotheses. Firstly, that it is possible to create an exit from the Shiftspace by visualising it in a particular way. Secondly, that, combined with the existing entrance into the Shiftspace, this can be used to form a bridge between two locations in our space-time. The data supports both hypotheses."

There was more, but I stopped reading. I felt fifteen again: inadequate, undermined, insignificant. I had not given myself account of it, but somewhere at the back of my mind an ugly thought had been festering: I had begun to nurture the idea that my theories would buy me recognition and fame enough not only to escape Mum's shadow, but to eclipse it with my own. Now I was looking at a paper dated fourteen years old that not only made the same claims, but tested and proved them.

"You didn't publish this," I whispered, unable to control my voice.

Mum shook her head.

"Why?"

She gestured at the paper again. "Just read it."

"The data supports both hypotheses," I read again, "However, the hypotheses also imply that someone must remain within the Shiftspace for the duration of the bridge, exerting sustained effort to visualise the exit. This effectively turns them into what we may call a Shiftslave, raising many of the ethical ramifications we typically attach to other forms of slavery. It also raises significant safety concerns: what happens to the Shiftslave or to those using a Shiftspace bridge if the exit is lost and cannot be re-established?"

I half-threw, half-dropped the paper towards Mum. I felt faint, steadied myself on the corner of her desk, then gave up and slowly sank to the floor, pressing my back against the wood of the desk hard enough for it to rake my spine.

I knew I was not thinking rationally, but it felt like she had anticipated my every move, had planned for it and closed it off years before I had even thought of making it. The anger I had kindled on my way here spilled over into tears of frustration, a sense of bitter futility. It seemed to me that no matter what I did, I could not untether myself from her dominance.

I sat on the floor, staring without recognition at a wall of books with Mum's name on them, my back to her.

"You and I can see this isn't just about the academic freedom of Shiftscience," she said. "If the Empire gets hold of this research, they will want to commercialise and militarise it no matter the risks or the human cost."

There was something about her choice of the conjunction 'you and I'—perhaps the pitiful concession of it, the morsel of

credit she was willing to throw my way—
that brought back all my venom in a
sudden surge. I lost control of myself.

"Tell me something," I said, still sat on
the floor staring ahead of me. "Do you cry
and scream when you're alone, like you
used to?"

It was a low and ugly move, but I had
made it and I was determined to play it
out.

"Do you try to tear your skin off and
scratch the walls when no one is looking?
Do you have anyone to cover it up for you,
to make excuses and keep the place in
order, like Dad used to do?"

She did not reply, so I got up, turned
around to look at her. Her face was still,
but pale as chalk. She gripped her chair
with white-knuckled intensity, squeezing
so hard I could hear her skin creak
against the varnish.

"Do your colleagues know how
unstable you are? That you haven't been
right for fifteen years? That all of this," I
waved a hand at the shelves around me,
"Was dreamt up by a sick mind?"

After a long moment, our eyes locked
but nothing passing between them, she
drew one long, deep breath and relaxed
her grip on the chair.

"I think we are done here," she said quietly.

After I returned from Morton I locked myself away in my dormitory in Arwall and did not attend any teaching for two months. A fortnight into my seclusion, Jacob came to visit to make sure I was alright. He found me dishevelled and sleep-deprived, surrounded by every available library text on Shiftscience, various diagrams, scribbled notes, and calculations pinned to my walls and laid out on the floor, one on top of the other in a collage of mad science. I briefly explained that I was working in a new direction suggested by my earlier hypotheses and a conversation with Mum. I appeared calm and focused, despite my exhaustion and dishevelment, and I was obviously entirely absorbed in study, so he left satisfied.

At the end of the two months I had written a paper. Maybe it was all that time with little food, sleep, and too much work, or perhaps I sensed the repercussions it would have, but I decided to forego the usual dry scientific titles in favour of something more lyrical: "A Bridge through the Void".

Based on supposition and extrapolation from existing theory and data, I proposed methods to create and hold open a bridge through the Shiftspace. My proposal still required someone to host the bridge—a Shiftslave, in Mum's terminology. It was a point of ethics that she had explored at length, but which I ignored entirely. Nor did I factor in the risks in the event that a host was unable to visualise, or to continue visualising, an exit.

Looking back, it pains me to admit that I simply did not care about these things. What mattered to me was the desire for recognition, the need to make my own mark on Shiftscience. The irony that my findings were identical to Mum's unpublished draft in almost every respect spurred me on rather than held me back. I told myself it mattered that I had developed my theories independently, without assistance or feedback. Nonetheless, the similarities frustrated me. It was all I could do to convince myself to focus on the immediate gains from publication, the platform it would give me for further study that would eventually render Mum's broader research programme obsolete.

I made a copy of the paper and placed it in an envelope addressed to the Scientific Oversight Office, the arm of the state's censorship. I had considered Jacob's and Mum's concerns about governmental interference in Shiftscience and rejected them. They seemed to me like short-sighted conservativism, a risk aversion that came with age rather than reason. I was desperate to collaborate with the Empire if it could launch my reputation as quickly as it had Mum's.

I remember very clearly my walk to the Office. The heavy Arwall air was cut through with the frosty breeze of an early spring morning. A haze hung over the streets, and through it the streetlights appeared like lighthouses, daisy-chained into the distance. I ignored the five-storey stone edifices around me and imagined I was crossing some vast archipelago, each island marked by its own flickering orange glow.

A motor-carriage rolled past, the wooden cabin swaying between two pairs of suspension rods like a bow-legged insect. Two policemen strolled in the opposite direction, their steel-capped boots echoing into the street. Despite what I was walking towards, I felt serene, almost weightless, giddy with excitement. Later, I would feel only the abrasive weight of guilt and regret.

The raid came three days after I had left the paper at the Scientific Oversight Office. I was in one of Jacob's lectures. The irregular tap-and-hiss of chalk against the large board and the steady baritone cadence as he narrated the progress of his calculations were suddenly interrupted by a rising murmur. I looked up from my notes. The other students were arguing in hushed, nervous voices and pointing outside. Through the tall windows of the lecture theatre, out on the green of the Institute grounds, I could see six groups of figures in long coats and dark berets spill out of black motor-carriages. One, a tall, heavy-set woman with short fair hair, got out last and separately from the others. She looked around, barked an inaudible order, and then joined the group headed towards our building. The others dispersed around the campus. Moments later I heard the muffled echo of their march through the corridors, growing louder and sharper until it seemed like the striking of a hammer.

I glanced over at Jacob and found his eyes on me. Something in my expression must have confirmed his suspicions, because he looked away in bitter disappointment. Suddenly he seemed composed, resigned even, and he began to wipe chalk from his hands and gather his notes. I wondered later how many years he had spent in fear of this kind of visit.

The double doors to the lecture theatre swung open with a clang and four figures filed in, led by the fair-haired woman. I and the others looked around nervously as two took position at the back of the theatre and two at the front. All were armed.

"Professor Lukash?" The woman addressed him. The weight of her voice matched her frame.

He nodded.

"Undergraduate Shiftscience?"

"Final year." His voice was small but steady.

"You and the students here are under arrest." She swept her gaze over the lecture theatre, took each of us in for just a moment. I could not say if she knew who I was.

"The order comes by emergency imperial edict, so I do not need to tell you the charges until you are brought into custody. Form a line and accompany me outside, where you will board a motor-carriage. I have the authority to shoot anyone who resists arrest or breaks file."

Jacob was silent for a few seconds, as if waiting for one of us to speak up.

"Student politics isn't what it used to be," he smiled. "May I see the papers?"

There is a rumour now that staff and students were shot during the raid. It is not true; there may have been violence—I saw some bloodied heads when they were transporting us—but no one was killed. The other five military groups raided the rest of the Shiftscience student body and staff at the same time. Every ongoing lecture and seminar was disrupted, and individuals were arrested in their offices and homes. Later I heard that similar operations were carried out simultaneously in Palaja and New Leven, the only other cities in the world with Shiftscience programmes. I told myself that it would not have been possible to effect this level of coordination in just three days. Given that Palaja and New Leven are outside imperial jurisdiction, I suspected that the plan for the raids had been worked out months in advance; it just needed a catalyst to be put into action. It was likely true, but it did not make me feel any better.

At the Scientific Oversight Office I had had the romantic notion that after I submitted my paper, I—I alone, an unrecognised genius of Shiftscience— would be approached to develop the bridge through the void promised in my paper. But the cold gunpoint reality of my situation and the misery I had inflicted on others had a sobering effect. I stared wide-eyed, shocked into passivity, as I was first jostled against the other students in one of the carriages, then spent two days in a holding cell, then finally was transferred to solitary confinement in what I later learned was Centre 17, a transit jail for political prisoners. I spent three months there without any account of the charges I was held under—a violation of imperial law, but I learned a common one: the prosecution needed time to gather evidence and find a charge to fit it.

Despite the uncertainty of my situation, I was relatively comfortable: I had a bed and a chair in a white-brick cell large enough for me to cross in three paces, with a wide slit for a window at the top of one wall. If I grabbed the edge and pulled myself up, I could see waves at the end of a long stretch of sand, cresting like a myriad folding hands, breaking against the mass of the sea before merging on the horizon into the blue-grey of the sky. At night the flicker of a distant lighthouse reminded me of my walk to the Scientific Oversight Office. It left a sour taste in my mouth.

I was not visited during this time and was given only trivial reading material. I could not complain; having something to occupy me, however basic, kept me sane. My meals—served three times a day—were delivered through a small flap in the centre of the cell door that locked from the outside and was also used to check that I was not attempting anything prohibited. I was not; the isolation and the relative comfort and idleness provided ample opportunity to reflect on the things I had done, to imagine the consequences, to try to come up with solutions, and this consumed me entirely.

On my best days, I fancied that the Empire had captured and held us to establish without interference a government monopoly on Shiftscience applications. If no one had access to Shiftscientists, then no one could affect imperial designs. I was convinced that once these designs were irrevocably in motion, we would all be released and allowed to carry on like nothing had happened. On my worst days I imagined that we were the test subjects for the theories I had developed in my paper, each of the Shiftscience scholars and students used as hosts for the Shiftspace bridges I had theorised—turned into Shiftslaves. All the time—on good and bad days—I was overcome with guilt. I was restless in that way one gets about things one has a responsibility for but no control over. The worry took its toll: despite the lack of exercise and the reasonable diet, I lost weight, my hair was streaked with premature grey, and new lines found their way into my skin like the imprints of a blunt knife pressed too hard and for too long.

Some time in my fourth month in Centre 17, I had my first and last visitor. It is difficult to express the emotions I felt when the cell door opened and I saw Mum in her usual black skirt and jacket, standing alone and with a slight smile curling her lips. An upswell of the guilt and remorse I had lived with for three months, but also relief, hope, the joy of seeing another human being, perhaps even something approximating a familial bond.

Mum watched me silently for a short while, then nodded to someone outside the cell, came in, closed the door, and sat across from my bed on the lone chair.

"How did you get away from the raids?" I asked. It was the first thing that came into my head and I said it without thinking.

Mum winced. "Is that really what you'd like to talk about?"

She paused. I said nothing.

"I had a notion of what you might do after our last meeting," she said. "I had no way to stop you, so I assumed the worst and prepared for it. You didn't disappoint."

"You didn't help it," I bristled.

"No," to my surprise she nodded, "I didn't."

We sat in silence for a few moments. Her admission weighed awkwardly between us. My eyes were fixed on the floor but I could feel Mum studying me, examining the damage three months in solitary confinement had done. As much as our last meeting felt like an audition, so this felt like a post-mortem. I shuddered.

"I need you to know that I came as quickly as I could," she said at last in a small, quiet voice. I was incredulous: was this the start of an apology?

"It took time to find where they were holding you and to negotiate terms," she continued. "I have friends in the major newspapers and in several government positions, which is how I am able to be here at all."

There was another pause. I looked up from the floor; Mum's eyes were glazed over and her jaw set tight, as if she were consciously clenching her teeth. It was too difficult to imagine that she was holding herself back from tears.

"I've negotiated your release," she added.

I was not sure how I felt. I brushed down the creases in my trousers to distract myself with the motion.

"You said 'terms'?"

"Yes," she sighed. A long pause. "I've agreed to run the imperial Shiftslavery programme."

I looked back at the floor, my eyes darting to find something in the uniform grey of the concrete that I could fixate on so I would not have to think about this. It went against everything Mum had planned for Shiftscience, against her entire career of keeping the government away from her discoveries and their misuse. I ran my hands over my trousers again.

"But this isn't something I can do alone," she added. "I need your help."

A circle appeared at my feet, painted a darker grey than the rest of the concrete floor. Then another, then two at once. I wiped at my cheeks and nodded.

I found out that Mum had begun relocating her laboratory as soon as I had left her cottage in Morton on my last visit. Her public profile and years of influence in government meant that no one had dared to interfere with her even as the rest of the Shiftscience programme had been arrested.

She moved to Symoni, in South Coral, about as far away from the Empire's influence as she could get without running out of friends or people who owed her favours. The Empire had a delicate relationship with Coral that it did not want to upset and, until Mum's arrival, Coral had no organised Shiftscience programme, so she was confident that we would be safer there than anywhere else.

Mum took us back to Arwall and we chartered a small steamboat to Symoni. She had negotiated my release as an explicit condition of her involvement in Shiftslavery, but the authorities refused to recognise this formally in her contract, so she preferred to keep a low profile during our travel. A private ship also left us at liberty to discuss Shiftscience without fear of being overheard.

The voyage took six weeks, largely through waters outside the Empire's jurisdiction. In the mornings, if it was sunny, I would sit out on the deck and read old newspapers that the captain—a well-meaning man in his sixties who, remarkably, did not seem to know who Mum was—had collected before the voyage. He did not care for the sensationalist fearmongering, as he called it, but they made good kindling for the furnaces that powered the ship's engine and he did not mind if I leafed through them before they were burned.

The rustle of the pages in the fresh breeze and the distant squawks of occasional sea birds put me at ease, but I was melancholy at the sight of the sea—it reminded me of the view from my cell window in Centre 17.

In the afternoons and evenings, I studied with Mum. From the beginning she made it clear that she had no intention of supporting Shiftslavery in the long-term, but that we had to put ourselves in a position of sufficient knowledge and trust to dismantle it. Awareness of this objective kept me focused and motivated, even if her lessons left me ambivalent. On one hand, they were a revelation; Mum moved through Shiftscience with a confidence and speed that Jacob could not hope to match, knew things he had only guessed at, and proposed and rejected theories with a confidence that was not weighed down by fear of peer review. For the first time in my life I could see for myself how she had earned her reputation. On the other hand, she seemed to be holding something back. Even when the lessons were ostensibly presented as freeform, I sensed an underlying structure. It was as if Mum had crafted a secret curriculum that was shaping me towards something other than what she was willing to discuss openly. I could not guess what it might be, but I did not confront her for fear of destabilising the relative semblance of family life that we now had. This sense of secrecy kept us at a distance from each other, despite everything we had been through.

We arrived in Symoni at the end of summer. With each day closer to Coral, the sun seemed to shine brighter and longer, until the heat was so strong that I could not tolerate my mornings on the deck and spent them instead in my cabin with the porthole open and the door left ajar to attract a draught. In Symoni's harbour—moored downwind of its famous fish markets and incense parlours—the heat was compounded by a stench that made me gag for an hour before I was able to acclimate to it.

Mum's new laboratory was in a three-storey townhouse at the end of a palm-shaded avenue in a quiet residential part of the city that did not see much traffic; it would help maintain a low profile. Apart from the bright yellow wallpaper and the extravagant glass light fixtures, the décor was similar to what I remembered of her cottage in Morton: frugal, minimalist, devoid of imagination. But after the unbearable brightness and heat outside, it felt like an oasis of darkness and cool.

"Welcome to your new home," Mum said. "Get settled and then meet me on the top floor. I need to show you something."

Her tone put me on edge. My suspicion that she had been working towards a secret agenda returned with tenfold intensity. I gave her the same long, appraising look I had given her in Morton. It was not comforting; she had aged terribly in the last few months, clearly under the weight of a large and unshifting burden.

She noticed that I was assessing her and tried to smile in reassurance, but it only made things worse. In all the time I had known her, Mum had never been one for polite comforts. "You make your choices and don't look back, or you don't make them at all," she used to say when I was little.

"What is it?" I said.

She sighed. "Well, you might as well come up now if you are going to ask."

We climbed two flights of stairs and Mum pushed open a wooden door to a space that filled the entirety of the attic. A pair of skylights cast uneven, trembling light shafts. Dust motes danced between two rows of chest-high wooden tables stacked with equipment. From what I could tell, most were measuring stations and calculation engines. Their dials glittered like cat eyes. Between the rows of tables, partially covered by a yellowing sheet, was something that looked like a metalwork arch or doorway, about a head taller than me and wide enough for one person. I don't know why, perhaps it was the fact that it was hidden, but looking at it put me ill at ease. I walked to the arch and removed the cover. With the whole contraption exposed, I could see that it was a long metal tube bent into a U-shape and inserted into two stands bolted to the floor. Countless cables, wires and antennae wound around the length of the tube like the vines of creeper plants. They trailed loosely from connectors dotted sporadically around the arch, across the floor and up to the tables and the equipment there. I looked at Mum. She had remained standing near the door.

"I call it a Shiftlens," she said. "It thins the boundary between our reality and the Shiftspace, which induces the Shiftspace to manifest within the span of the lens. The encasement also means I can monitor it precisely. If you want to put it crudely, it's a gate attached to a calculation engine."

Shiftscience orthodoxy was that no one could exert any control over the way the Shiftspace manifested; it did so when it wanted and as far as it wanted in a handful of known places. During our voyage, Mum had been explicit that I could enter any values for location and dimension I wanted in my calculations, which I had assumed was because they were unimportant to her lessons. Now I realised it was because she had been gradually steering me towards a new way of looking at the problem.

"Why didn't you just tell me about this?" I said wearily.

"A number of reasons," she shrugged. "It's easier to believe in something and to work with it when you already understand the theory. But mainly I didn't want you to know this too early in case anything happened to us during the voyage."

For a moment I felt a surge of the resentment I had felt in Morton—still untrusted and unworthy of Mum's most closely guarded work. But whether through the months of incarceration or the weeks aboard a ship together, I no longer had the energy to sustain that feeling.

"What else haven't you told me?"

She walked towards the Shiftlens, ran a hand over it absently, then looked up at me. For some reason it was the first time I realised that I was taller. She seemed suddenly and strangely vulnerable.

"Your paper is essentially correct," she said and I couldn't help the fleeting sense of self-satisfaction. "But you assume that the Shiftspace will admit of an indefinite number of hosts, all visualising their own exit points, all exchangeable for other hosts. That's understandable, given the state of mainstream Shiftscience, but it's not right."

Mainstream Shiftscience. Moments ago I would have balked at the term—hadn't Mum's   work   defined   mainstream

Shiftscience?—but the existence of the Shiftlens suggested that she had been working on her own agenda for some time.

"The Shiftspace is a kind of parasite," she continued. "I believe that fundamentally it's just a void that cannot be touched or entered or filled. It's a nothing in almost the literal sense of that word. But when it opens, it looks for a symbiont. To keep the symbiont within it, to keep them comfortable, the Shiftspace tries to mimic its natural habitat."

"This is textbook Shiftscience," I shrugged, "The Shiftspace wants to keep the entry from our reality open so it can better mimic our environment and attract additional hosts, which sustain it somehow."

"Not *hosts*—plural," she shook her head, "*host*—singular. It forms a bond with the first person through the entry, and, as far as I can tell, that bond is in place for life. I've always supposed that it feeds off organic matter—perhaps the brain waves we give off, or our pheromones, or something else—I don't know. The point is that the Shiftspace benefits from having as many of us inside as possible. But there is only ever one host. That's where your paper goes wrong.

At best you can generate just one exit point from the Shiftspace, and you'd better make sure you never lose your host."

She let me think about that for a moment. In the silence I noticed one of her old mannerisms: she ran one arm over the other and pinched at her skin as she did so. It looked like she was trying to adjust a sleeve or peel away a carapace. It had terrified me when I was a child; now I only found it repulsive.

"Why do you do that?' It spoke to how much we had been through in the last few weeks that I felt able to ask the question.

She looked down in surprise. "Oh, that." She trailed off. "That first expedition, fifteen years ago: I was the first to enter the Shiftspace. And, well, I already said that it bonds with the first one through."

I stared in horror. "Are you saying that it's sentient? That it's some sort of organism bonded to you?"

"No, not in the way we usually understand sentient organisms anyway. It just has a certain basic degree of... *tropism*. Yes, I suppose that word will do here. It latches on to a host and mimics its habitat the way a flower knows to open towards the sun: it's a primal reflex, not sentient intent."

Her face caught somewhere between a smile and a shudder. After so many years of seeing her seemingly in control, it was difficult to come to terms with how much of it had been pretence.

"As for the bond between us," she continued, "It's less sinister than you might imagine. I feel the Shiftspace beside me every moment, even when it is closed, but it's not like someone watching or dictating my actions. It's more like a calling to return to it, a yearning to get back to an entry point, re-enter it, and never leave."

She looked back at me and her eyes suddenly refocused and held their usual calm, balanced detachment. I realised that it was a defence mechanism—for all these years not a mask of superiority or power, but a wall between whatever was inside her and the outside world.

I gazed at her wide-eyed in disbelief. Fifteen years paired with that nothingness, unable to extricate herself, bound to the science she had founded through more than just ambition or curiosity, unwilling to tell anyone in case...in case what?

"Why didn't you tell anyone? For all this time?"

"I did." She smiled. "I told your father as soon as I came back from that expedition and understood what had happened."

I doubt I could have expected a more surprising admission.

"Dad knew all this time?"

"He did," she nodded. "We agreed that the information was too dangerous to us to make public. We decided to keep it secret until I found the means to break the symbiosis."

We decided, *we* agreed, dangerous to *us*. There was something like a family there after all, once.

"But you never did." My voice was hoarse.

"No." Mum looked over at the Shiftlens. "The Shiftlens was my attempt. It was supposed to act as a substitute for a live host. Fifteen years of rebuilding and fine-tuning suggest I was wrong. It can open the Shiftspace, but it cannot replace me as a host. There is only one way out."

Mercifully, she left it unsaid. She had already explained that the symbiont needed to die to break the link with the Shiftspace. It did not bear repeating.

"I think your father came to terms with that years ago," she added bitterly, "he said farewell long before I could say it."

A silence settled between us. I stared dumbly at the Shiftlens, as if it held all the answers, or perhaps because in some abstract way it represented the Shiftspace and Mum's attempt at liberating herself from it. She had called it a gate, after all. Within a few minutes my knowledge of Shiftscience and my past had been rearranged into an entirely new worldview. It was humbling and it was overwhelming. Above all I tried to make sense of the new perspective I had on Mum and Dad as a family. It felt awkward somehow, unpractised, forced, like I was peering back at two people who did not know how to be with each other.

"Listen," Mum said eventually, "Why don't we pick this up tomorrow? We'll both feel better when we've had some sleep."

Sleep eluded me. The bed—in a small room on the ground floor—was too soft and the air too close. I got up, walked barefoot to the window and threw it open.

A gentle breeze drifted in from a small garden planted thick with white flowers that glowed pale in the bright moonlight. Swarms of insects unknown to me darted amongst the stems and settled on the petals. The breeze covered my skin in goosebumps. I padded back to the bed and climbed under the thin sheet, took a deep breath of the cool night air.

I was exhausted, but my mind worked frantically to reassemble old information in light of new, and kept me awake. Assumptions, memories, long-held opinions were reworked like a song played on unfamiliar instruments: different timbre and pitch, new harmonies, but recognisably the same. I stared up with unblinking eyes. Images from my childhood, my Mum's face, Dad's, passed before me like a slideshow projected onto the ceiling. It was difficult to comprehend that instead of a decade of living distant and separate lives, my parents had followed a pact to protect each other. That despite Mum's mounting success and reputation in Shiftscience, her primary goal—to break her symbiosis with the Shiftspace—was a source of constant and repeated failure. I admired her resilience, but then I supposed that perseverance was easier when forfeit was not an option. I had better perspective on Dad's descent into bitterness and spite; he had waited ten years for Mum to unmake the choice she had made, to return to her family, even as that family withered away. They saw less and less of each other, I grew up, and what he waited for became with every year less important, more abstract, something he believed in by rote, something he believed he ought to believe.

After a while I became aware of a low humming sound and a vibration that seemed to penetrate the whole building. I got up again and leaned out of the window. The sound was almost inaudible now, but I could feel the vibration through my feet, which meant the source was likely inside the house. I wondered if Mum was still working in the laboratory, and I imagined the Shiftlens, thrumming with energy as it held a space of black emptiness within its span. It occurred to me, suddenly and unbidden, that Mum's symbiosis with the Shiftspace put a halt to any imperial plans for Shiftslavery. She had confirmed that the theory and method I had developed in "A Bridge through the Void" were in most respects correct, but until her existing link with the Shiftspace could be severed, the Empire would be unable to use another host. They would be unable to force that host to remain within the Shiftspace and demand that they hold a bridge open by visualising some exit point.

I had a sudden, awful feeling somewhere at the core of me, a premonition I could not ground in anything concrete Mum had done or said, but it arrived with dreadful certainty all the same. At once I thought I knew the reason for the low humming vibration through the building, what it signified.

I raced out of my room and up the stairs. My nightshirt and hair flailed around me and my bare feet slapped against the wooden floors. By the time I reached the bottom of the staircase to the lab the vibration and the humming had ceased, and I was running through a deathly quiet filled only with foreboding and the echo of my footfall.

I slammed open the door to the lab. A wave of heat buffeted me. The heat grew more intense as I walked towards the Shiftlens. I reached out and almost immediately jerked my hand back in pain. The Shiftlens's surface was hot enough to brand the skin. I could see parts of it glowing pink and turning a faint amber as it cooled.

I glanced around. The lab was empty. The moonlight streamed through the skylights and cast everything in silver outline like a heliotype negative. Nothing was out of place from earlier in the day, except that on one table there was a stack of paper with a single sheet next to it. Hesitantly, anxious, I picked up the stack and placed it under one of the skylights. In the moonlight I could just make out the title on the first page: "A Bridge through the Void". I recognised it as the copy I had left with the Scientific Oversight Office five months ago.

I should have guessed that the authorities would consult Mum after they received my paper. I wondered how much say she'd had in the political decisions they had taken. Either way, the fact that for months she could not find where I was imprisoned suggested that things had not gone according to her plans.

I looked over to the single sheet of paper. My lips were dry. I ran my tongue over them and found that I was struggling to breathe. I read the note.

"The basic principles of Shiftscience extend to the Shiftlens. It can create a new entrance into the Shiftspace, but the entrance will remain open only as long as there is a host inside.

"You are the legal owner of this building and you have the knowledge to use the equipment here. I also give you a list of people—the teachers and fellow students captured with you—whom I couldn't find. What you do with all this is up to you; I can finally give you that choice. Just remember: make it and don't look back, or don't make it at all. Love, Mum."

It read like a note to pick up the groceries, like it wasn't the first time Mum had told me she loved me, like it wasn't a farewell. I looked back at the silent, cooling metal of the Shiftlens, around at the empty lab.

She had left it unsaid because she knew that I would understand. She was gone. I did not need to see evidence or learn the grisly details of her passing to know it with certainty. Her connection to the Shiftspace and her grip on Shiftscience were broken. For the first time the Shiftspace was without a host, and Shiftscience without a patron and master. The choice of what to do with this knowledge was my inheritance. Strangely, there was no part of me that needed to deliberate what to do with it. In some way I had always known it—I was a satellite, finally freed from its orbit.

I took the note, but left my paper where it was. With a bit of effort I tore out two cables from a pair of calculation engines and rubbed the exposed ends together until they sparked. The paper caught fire —a small flame that somehow looked like an inferno in the dark room and cast wild shadows across the walls.

I hurried downstairs, dressed, collected the luggage I had not had a chance to unpack and stepped out into the street.

A stream of charcoal grey smoke and the occasional lick of flame poured from the attic and some of the second-storey windows. I could hear a few panicked shouts and the sound of running. A man dashed past me with a bucket but did not pay me any attention.

I looked towards the seafront. The ship that had brought me here from Arwall would still be moored in the harbour. I clutched the list of names Mum had left me and set off towards it, never looking back.

See Andrei Pechalin's story "Heritage" online at Metaphorosis.
If you liked it, leave a comment. Authors love that!
Remember to subscribe to our e-mail updates so you'll know when new stories are posted.

About the story

I grew up in a family with quite a few high achievers: actors, journalists, engineers, etc. That puts some pressure on you to be something – you want to be successful as quickly as possible, almost so you can tick that off and move on. It can lead to bad decision-making, and I made some mistakes in my late teens and early 20s (although none as drastic as the protagonist's, I hasten to add!). So I guess that's where the core idea – how do you choose to live your life in light of your heritage? – came from.

I've written a few stories that are perhaps too obsessed with world-building detail and that introduce too many characters, so I wanted to do something more stripped down and focused on what makes those characters work. That's how I ended up with just the protagonist and her mother. After a while I realised I didn't have to name them, which for me underscores that this is about them as people. It also shows, I hope, that it's possible to tell a story with strong female leads without ever mentioning their names.

The idea of the Shiftspace is really just the old trope of parallel dimensions, but I've given it some odd properties to make it weird and a bit dark. This works better with the overall mood of the story and the ending. I actually introduced the Shiftspace in an earlier story, 'Jurisdiction', where it's used for extraordinary rendition, but I had to expand the lore significantly here.

I also play a lot of video games and there have been an increasing number of stories focused on parent-child relationships (maybe the medium is maturing, or maybe game developers are just getting older). It's difficult to ignore *The Last of Us* and the last *God of War*, for example. I didn't consciously reference these, but perhaps they shaped some of the overall direction subconsciously.

A question for the author

Q: What is the scariest or most disturbing story you've ever read?

A: Bret Easton Ellis' *American Psycho*. It has the most horrifying and gratuitously extreme violence I've ever had to imagine, and makes the film look like a family blockbuster by comparison.

About the author

Andrei Pechalin has lived in England for over 20 years after emigrating from Russia. He studied law and analytic philosophy when he was younger and now works in higher education. He is convinced that video games have something interesting and important to contribute to narrative form, and will write one someday, right after that novel he keeps putting off.

www.pechalin.com, @APechalin

Tower of Mud and Straw

Yaroslav Barsukov

IV. The Tower

This is the final part of Yaroslav Barsukov's novella, *Tower of Mud and Straw*. Parts 1, 2, and 3 ran in September, October, and November 2020. What has gone before:

Faced with the prospect of greatness, Shea makes a deal with his own conscience: he knows a way to save the tower. He and Aidan travel to Shea's old home in Musk Valley to retrieve the 'tulips' buried there.

It is revealed that it was Shea's sister who coined the 'tulips' moniker. Together, they used to run a furniture workshop in Musk Valley, and she planned to use the Drakiri's anti-gravity devices to increase the production efficiency. The plan backfired horribly, killing Lena and another worker and destroying the workshop. Shea buried the 'tulips' she'd bought under the workshop's remains.

Shea and Aidan retrieve the 'tulips' and take them to Owenbeg. Lena, who's previously offered Shea to leave Owenbeg with her, perceives this as a betrayal. She's furious. She claims she's never really cared for Shea, and promises to confess their affair to the duke.

1

How many steps can a person take until the course of events becomes irreversible —fifty? A hundred? In his mind, Shea counted Lena's: now she rushed through the corridor, now she passed through the criss-cross shadows that had slipped from the window grates.

She'd said she would destroy him, but he was already a man caught under the rubble: one part of him would've given everything to run after her, the other paralyzed, repeating the same word. *Guilty.*

Guilty, but at least he would have power; if that would be worth the cost—at all.

What would he have told her, had he followed her? There was nothing he could tell her.

Outside, a chickadee let out a 'dee-dee-dee'. He remembered his and Lena's visit to the Drakiri settlement, the garlands, the roundabout spinning sunlight into black hair—and fatigue, gray, featureless, rolled over him.

"It's too late, little bird," he said. "One's dead, and I've betrayed the other one."

The sound of his own voice finally allowed him to move, and he stepped out into the corridor.

The courtyard stood deserted save for Aidan's men—creations of a sculptor too drunk to have been allowed anywhere near a chisel—and Brielle. She was still discussing something with them, waving her hand at the cart loaded with black egg-shaped things.

"I need to talk to you," Shea said.

She turned her whole body to him, beaming like a child on New Year's Day.

"Thirty-two devices, Shea. Thirty-two. You're a genius."

"Please. I want to talk."

He took her aside, under a creeper stretching its feelers across the wall.

"I understand it's awkward, but I've absolutely no one to turn to. It's about Lena."

"Okay, an interesting start. I didn't expect that, to be honest. What kind of *advice* are you looking for?"

"She's an acquaintance of yours, right?"

"Barely. I mean, we're both part of the duke's entourage, but we almost do not cross paths otherwise."

"She's going to confess our affair to the duke."

Brielle's eyes widened. "What the... What happened between you two?"

"This happened." He pointed at the cart. "She believes in an old Drakiri legend, another tower emerging when ours reaches a certain height. Something like that."

"*Emerging?*"

"Yes, from hell. Don't ask. She was happy when she learned the tower was about to crumble."

"What?" Brielle's face went one shade paler. "You told her? You've *told* her? We've agreed to keep it between ourselves —"

"It was like..." *The lovemaking, the angel, the olive branch.* "Listen, she wasn't going to tell anyone."

"Did you tell her I'd made a mistake in the calculations?"

"No, of course not. Why would I tell her that?"

"It's important to me, Shea. Did you tell her I'd made a mistake?"

"No! Besides, it's not relevant right now. Right now she's, let's say, extremely angry with me."

"Because you've brought in fresh devices."

"Because I've brought in the tulips."

"Why don't you talk to your friend from the capital?"

"Because he *worries me*, Brielle. He has certain tendencies... I don't trust him."

"Wow." She glanced back at Aidan's goons. "Oi! Don't touch those things, fellas! Sorry, Shea. I assume you've tried to reason with her?"

"*How* would I reason with her? You can't imagine what this legend means to her. *I* knew it and I didn't say anything to her, about going to Musk Valley and retrieving the tulips. Now she won't listen to me. I've betrayed her."

"Stop being melodramatic." Brielle chewed on her lip and looked up at the sky. "Listen, I need to take care of the devices before dark. Have you considered the fact she's got as much to lose as you do? Her relationship with the duke we all know nothing about and we all suspect exists?"

She's right. Of course she's right. You overreacting idiot.

"I don't think anything will happen, Shea. I think she's just mad at you. This'll blow over. I'm no expert on relationships, but I would wait a few days and try talking to her again. If she's still mad by then, I'll talk to her myself, I promise."

"Thank you," he said. "You know, I can't say we're friends in the strictest sense of the word..."

"I know." Brielle smiled. "More like battle comrades."

"Yeah, but I mean, I just want to say— thank you, Brielle."

"Before this gets awkward, I'll dash off and attend to those idiots—otherwise they'll blow themselves up. Stop worrying about things, you shoulder way too much blame."

He watched her figure sail up to the cart, then turned and went back into the castle.

2

Brielle turned out to be wrong.

They came for him during the night, and they weren't exactly courteous. The dream in which he'd been cutting a rotten grapevine collapsed as he spat out caked dust from the rags someone had shoved into his mouth. He blinked: a person—or persons—stood behind an oil lamp swinging in a blurred kaleidoscope. Darkness extended hands which yanked him out of bed. He tried to twist away, but they held him fast.

Shea kicked blindly, and a man cursed in a rich baritone, letting go of his right arm.

Free from the grip, his fist found something soft, probably the guy's guts. This prompted a grunt and another curse —but immediately, almost like the body's own sympathetic reaction, Shea's solar plexus flared up, and the world drowned in white sparks.

No more violence followed: they must've had orders not to leave any marks. They simply twisted his arms behind his back and dragged him out of his quarters.

From his new position, Shea could only see the floor tiles, but it was irrelevant: he had a hunch where they were headed.

Down, up, up, down, through a hallway.

A door threw open, and light bit into his eyes. The men who held his arms—he still wasn't sure, but there seemed to be three of them in total, two assailants and one who'd been responsible for the oil lamp—pushed him to his knees.

Legs swam into focus, stretching out of a night robe, sticks painted in varicose. Then came the rest, sitting on the edge of a grand four-poster bed, under a canopy filled with figures carrying swords and pitchforks.

"Ashcroft," the duke said. "Ashcroft."

He looked normal, even more controlled than usual: focused, spider-like eyes, hands gripping the knees as though calcified into them—but he didn't seem to be able to push out more than a single word.

"Ashcroft."

She was there, too, in her long black dress, staring out a window which couldn't have shown much apart from the torches down in the courtyard. Shea remembered the yellow room, how she'd seemed, in the same way, detached from whatever was happening around her.

"Lena," he said, and his solar plexus exploded again.

She didn't turn her head.

"Why don't you shut up for a change?" The duke's hand came alive and ran over his colorless lips. "You know, I did have a hunch something had happened between you two, Ashcroft. Still, I hoped common sense in you would prevail—forgetting how people always find ways of letting me down."

"Sorry to disappoint you."

Out of the corner of his eye, Shea saw the man on his right start a movement, but the duke made a dismissive grimace.

"Leave him be. It's a bit too late to feel sorry, Ashcroft, sincerely or otherwise."

"Hurt me, and you'll have a hell lot of explanation to do to Daelyn."

"Will I?" The duke smoothed down his hair as if preparing for a morning routine. "Remember, when you'd paraded in here, you didn't even know about the Drakiri devices—or the sabotage attempts. I tell my people to keep a lid on something—they do. They're loyal to me. That's what good leadership brings you."

Shea chuckled.

"Look at him," the duke said. "Look at him, Lena. Defiant to the end. I said *look at him!*"

She didn't move—in fact, she ceased all movement. She resembled a statue now.

"Anyway." The duke's palm touched his lips again, wiping the spit. "I've got a couple of ideas about you, Ashcroft. Both are marvelous, in their own way. One: we take you to the cellars and put your neck through a noose. Or two," he leaned forward, "these fine gentlemen here castrate you."

Shea felt blood rush away from his face. The walls came alive, bending around him, morphing into huge, cold fingers. The room shook.

"Your choice," the duke said.

"Lena." Shea tried to stand, but hands shoved him back into place. "Lena. Look at me."

Look at me. A small motion, barely noticeable: she dug her fingernails into her palms.

"So what will it be, Ashcroft?"

"Your Grace," the guy with the baritone said. "My boys and I are ready to do both."

The face above the night robe brightened, and for the first time since the yellow room, Shea saw an emotion other than anger or irritation pass through the duke's features.

"What a wonderful suggestion," he said. "Gosh. Absolutely splendid. Pull down his pants."

I've got a few seconds left. If I drop to the floor...

The entrance door creaked, and a voice called out, "Your Grace." The duke jerked in surprise. For a second, the pressure on Shea's shoulders weakened.

...I can sweep one of those bastards.

He threw himself on the stone tiles, rolled over, and drove his boot into the ankle of the guy to his left, who let out a short scream. In rapid succession, he glimpsed Aidan's face through the door, the canopy above the duke's bed, knuckles of a bear-shaped fist.

When the room stopped rocking, he and Aidan were on their knees next to each other.

"Exactly when we need a witness," the duke said. "What the hell are you doing here?"

"Your Grace, I just want to talk," said Aidan.

"What's the harm now?" The old man flexed his wrist as though considering shoving him between the ribs. "Let's hear it. What did you want to say?"

"Your Grace, before you do anything *irreversible*, you should know something about the Drakiri woman. That person isn't who you think she is."

"Meaning?"

"She's behind the sabotage attempts at the tower."

What is this nonsense?—but then Shea glanced at Lena. She no longer looked impartial, or distant, or trying to contain something. She took a step back from the window, eyes locked on Aidan.

"Very funny," the duke said. "Very, very funny. There were no sabotage attempts, my lord, Ashcroft himself proved it. Our workers couldn't handle the devices."

"Lord Ashcroft *theorized* unskilled labor was the problem. It was a good theory, too —however, only partially correct."

"Go on."

"She was using you, Your Grace, to get access to the tower. I have proof. My people have detained her fellow saboteurs."

His people—*Colm? Or did he bribe more?*

Lena shifted her gaze from Aidan to the duke, then to something behind Shea's back, then to Shea. And looking into her eyes, he was, again, a man split in two, one half sensing the tables reversed on the person who'd put him into this situation.

The other half though, a warmer and larger one, wished to cover her with his own body. The roundabout, the smile, the smell of strawberries. *I didn't lie*, he realized. What he felt here and now, on the floor of this hideous old man's room, was something beautiful.

"The witnesses are ready for your questioning, Your Grace," Aidan said.

"Aren't you going to say anything?" The duke half-turned to Lena. Having received no answer, he tsk'ed. "What's the motive?"

"That's what I didn't understand until recently, either," said Aidan. "It's no secret Drakiri aren't fond of the tower, but two days ago, Lord Ashcroft really opened my eyes. Apparently, they're prone to some kind of a doomsday superstition. How do you call it?" He pointed his chin at Lena. "The Mimic Tower?"

Still no answer, but she smiled—a sad, wise smile.

"So that's how it is." The duke lowered and shook his head. "Lena—I assume, by your silence, these allegations are at least partially justified?" The muscles in his jaw tightened. "All right, we'll consider the evidence."

At that moment, Shea saw with perfect clarity how the master's anger mirrored the servant's—the same detached rage Patrick had displayed against everything and everyone he considered an enemy, against the Dumians, against the 'capital types'.

"You want to punish someone—punish me, motherfucker," he said. "Leave her alone."

Aidan grabbed him by the arm. "Have you gone mad? Your Grace, he's simply—"

"Do whatever you've got to do. You wanted to punish me, so do it."

The duke collected himself.

Heavens, I've just doomed her. He'll get two for the price of one—

"Let Ashcroft go," the duke said. "Let both bastards go. But if you get wind of them talking to someone about this... In the meantime—"

Lena looked Shea in the eye and, with the same smile, mouthed a single-syllable word. Then, in one move, she tore at the hem of her dress, leaving an ugly ragged edge. The wave of heavy fabric fell, no longer constraining her movements.

She hurled herself at the window.

He bolted to his feet and dashed to the black rectangle edged with broken glass. Below, at the courtyard, in a pool of moonlit shards, a figure stretched like a bird. *Lena. Lena.*

But it wasn't over. The limbs twitched, and the figure stumbled to its feet. A step, another, a lurch forward, a stride.

Improbably, as though he observed events unfolding in reverse, she raced for the gate.

"Fucking Drakiri," the baritone said from the other window with a shade of admiration.

"What's happening? What's happening?" The duke's voice, high-pitched. "Is she alive? Go after her."

Lena dove under the gate, legs flashing so fast they were butterfly's wings in the torchlight.

"If I may, Your Grace," said Aidan. "She's probably headed for the construction site. I've already taken the liberty of alerting the people there."

Over the battlements, the tower was a shape someone had cut out from the sky. *No, no, no*, Shea thought.

"Lena!" The only things listening to him were the horizon and the stones in the castle walls.

He took three long strides across the room, pushing aside one of the duke's men, and darted out into the corridor.

He didn't know how he'd gotten to the gate, how he'd crossed the first mile of the fields—he only came to his senses when a string of bleak yellow emerged from the darkness ahead.

Wives, he remembered. *Fiancées. Lanterns for the foremen who're staying for the night.*

The lights picked out a tall, thin figure slurring past them.

"Lena!" He stumbled, fell, tore at the grass, jerked to his feet, sprinted. "Turn back. It's a trap."

But she was too far away, and of course she was too fast for him—a smudge moving at an inhuman speed. When he passed the women in linen cloaks, she was already only a rough outline, shrinking. When he finally reached the tower, there was only him.

Night hid in every little shadow between the bricks, and portals up in the circular wall, like eyes, metered out a glow which could've been starlight. Shea bent over, hands on his knees.

"Lena," he cawed—then, straightening, loudly, "Lena!"

The wind came and rustled the grass.

He put his foot on the first step leading into the tower's mouth when something moved against the sky: something plummeted from the opening directly to the left and above him. But it wasn't like the earlier fall, a bird breaking through the glass—this time, it was like a sack being thrown out, a useless, inanimate thing.

He couldn't run anymore; he had to make an effort not to fall.

It took him minutes to find the body: the night didn't care for things the way daylight did, all dark malt and caked-together shapes.

His fingers touched a wet spot on her left breast.

And when he raised her from the ground, wrapping his hand around her shoulders to bring her face to his chest, déjà vu washed over him—only, unlike the other Lena from his past, this one didn't call him by the name, didn't ask anything, didn't say she loved him.

Didn't say anything.

The roundabout in his memory stopped; under the garlands, she stepped back onto the pavement, smiling at the sun that tickled her nose.

"Thank you," he remembered her saying, and how he'd kissed her hand, and how nothing much mattered anymore.

You told me once, sis, that you could read hands. We were both kids, and it was all hogwash, of course—but to a child, things like fate do exist. I recall you said I would meet a beautiful, extraordinary woman whom I would fall in love with, and we would live happily ever after.

Funny how stuff from deep childhood holds sway over you. Looking back, now, I think I've always been waiting for the thing you'd told me to come true.

And hey, maybe you could read hands —that one time. Because the first part happened; it's the 'ever after' you got wrong.

3

There were crows—crows straddling the tree branches and crows in coats. The Drakiri settlement didn't look as rainbowy as it had the last time he'd been here, colors washed out by the rain into small puddles across the pavement.

Coming to think of it, the pavement wasn't as flat as he remembered it, either.

At the gates, he'd caught a glimpse of Brielle leaving in a carriage—but other than that, no faces from the castle.

A compact graveyard, maybe a hundred tombstones, filigree gratings: a place of refined sorrow. Shea passed under the iron archway that depicted two trees fused at the top. In an oak's shadow, a row of graves protruded from the ground like a procession of small animals that had gone somewhere but never made it.

He stopped.

A crowd of mourners surrounded a dark object he was afraid to look at. A man—a Drakiri—was making a speech, the wind only carrying individual words: 'beautiful', 'talented', 'loss'.

I shouldn't be here. I'm just as guilty as the people who'd killed her.

He caught the gaze of a tall woman in the front row; there was something familiar about her, something sweet and painful at the same time. Shea leaned against the oak, watching the graves, the Drakiri, the graphite clouds consume each other.

He brought himself to glance at Lena the moment before the coffin disappeared into the ground.

When everything was said and done and the people dispersed, the woman remained. She stretched her hand toward the fresh strip of earth. Then she looked at Shea again.

He straightened as she strolled up to him.

"You're Lord Ashcroft?"

He recognized the voice. "Yes." The pain of loss broke through the surface and sprouted. "I'm... I'm sorry we meet for the first time under these circumstances."

Her face went through a rapid cycle of grief: twitched, dropped, hardened. "I'm sorry, too."

He offered her an elbow, and they wandered past the graves.

"Lena told me you were a famous painter."

"She told me about you, too. I wanted to thank you. I think she loved you." Her voice broke for a second. "It was difficult to tell with her; she always hated showing weakness, and love can be one. But I think you were the only bright thing about her life at the castle."

The roundabout made one final swirl, and, risking a fall, he squeezed his eyes shut.

"How did she die?" she asked. "They told me next to nothing."

"They... they killed her. The duke's people at the tower. I think she was trying to destroy it, and I was trying to warn her, but it was all too late."

They walked in silence for a while.

"*You* taught her that story, about the Mimic Tower?" Shea asked.

"It's not a story. It's something, something real and terrifying." She seemed to trail off in thought. "She was a unique child. So talented. I never lost hope she would take up painting seriously."

"She said she painted a bit."

"Oh." As though sunlight had brushed across the woman's face, and the pain made Shea shrink inside: at that moment, she was an older version of her daughter. "Oh. She was a beautiful painter. Please, you need to come by sometime—I'll show you her works. Lena herself..." She broke off and pursed her lips.

Suddenly, even for himself, like a criminal who'd been holding out on a confession, he said, "I loved her, too."

The woman didn't respond. She nodded, either to his words or her own thoughts. Then she stopped and reached into her pocket. "She asked me to give something to you. 'You'll know when'—I only understand now what she meant."

Shea took an ornamental key from her and turned it over in his fingers. "What does it open?"

"I don't... I think it's from her quarters in the castle."

"Thank you."

"I would be grateful," she said, "I would be grateful if you could bring me something of hers."

4

The key began as a pair of hands entwined in the shape of a heart; the place where they connected to the stem so thin that Shea paused before the lock, afraid of breaking something beautiful and fragile.

Then he realized he'd already done that.

The keyhole let out a click.

Drakiri don't let strangers in, he remembered. *We have no records of where we came from, only that we'd arrived from elsewhere, and letting someone under your roof feels like sharing this vulnerability.*

The windows were leaded glass with shapes of clouds and wheat ears, orange lozenges here and there letting in rays of light, autumn on autumn. Fluid cornices above the windows mirrored the pointed arches which rested on spiral columns, creating a kind of a vestibule. Past them, drapes, orange too, fluttered on the walls like wings of an invisible insect.

A thin-legged writing desk stood slashed open, as did a wine cabinet, drawers on the floor, half of them smashed into splinters—somebody had been here already, either the duke's men or Aidan's.

Had they taken what she'd wanted him to find? Shea squatted and picked up, one by one, things scattered across the floor: a brooch. A muff.

Papers.

The sentences, in a free, floating handwriting, weren't in Drakiri. He shuffled through a few sheets to find what was apparently the beginning: *This won't be in my mother tongue because it's a diary of a different life, a life among different people.*

The pages were numbered, and in the setting sun through the orange lozenges, he crawled around the floor on all fours, trying to piece together what remained of her thoughts.

The duke...

The tower...

Patrick, Brielle, and the others...

That festival I've loved since my childhood...

The tower.

Next to one of the paragraphs stood a doodle of a face—his own.

'We rode on that thing, a thing for children, and I felt happy for the first time in a long while. I felt like a little girl. I may need to use him (do I? Maybe the situation will resolve itself before that?), and I'm torn. He may be my sailor. I don't want to lose that—in life, we aren't given many chances.'

Shea froze. Then he folded the pages in two, slowly, accurately. Ran his finger across the edge, feeling the paper fluffs crumble. Put the diary into his pocket.

Something boiled down his lungs, knocked at his throat, looked for a release.

He picked up the nearest drawer and hurled it into the wall. Another. And another, each next one with greater force, finally sliding into a scream, trying, but unable, to reach for the part of himself he wanted to hurt and make stop hurting.

He leaned his hands on the table and doubled over in dry sobs. *A proud, misguided child*, he thought. *I called her a proud, misguided child.*

The senses came back after a while: the smell of chipped wood, the room, the wheat ears, the drapes. His head felt the way it does when one catches a cold.

That was it. Somehow, it was not the funeral but reading her innermost thoughts that made him realize—really realize—that he would never see her again.

"Was it the diary, Lena? Did you want me to find it?"

His gaze fell on the door into the neighboring room.

She must've used it—the bedroom—for art practice. In the corner, a drawing table squatted, blank sheets of paper and pencils in a fine mess. Sketches occupied every inch of the walls, sketches—

Wait a second, not sketches. A sketch. They're all the same.

Or rather, they were of the same place: the clearing on the forested hillside where he and Lena had hunted and lost a deer.

Had the deer really vanished? he thought. 'I saw something, in a flash. Different colors,' she'd said.

He tore off a drawing and stared at it.

5

Brielle's face appeared in the crack between the door and the jamb.

"What is it, Shea?"

"May I come in?"

"I've been at the top of the tower all day. Installing the devices."

"Can you let me in?"

"I'm preparing for sleep."

"It's important."

"What isn't?" she said, stepping aside. "All right. You'll need to excuse a certain degree of messiness, though."

He didn't mind the clothes over the couch's back and cup rings on the table— it was everything else, the normal things, that, after *her* quarters, seemed bland and alien. Linen curtains, cornices and moldings he'd seen a thousand times.

"Remember, two days ago, I told you about the Mimic Tower?" he asked.

"Yes, you said it was a Drakiri superstition or something."

"What if it isn't?"

"Hmm?"

"Technologically, they're centuries ahead of us."

Brielle took a cup from the table—tea or coffee. "Doesn't mean they aren't..." She broke off.

"They aren't what? Human? If you think they are, go outside and hire a drikshaw."

"Doesn't mean they can't be prone to the same fear of the irrational as we are."

"Yes, but my point is, we won't be able to tell. We're children playing on the beach. *We* won't be able to tell their fear of irrational from legitimate concern."

"So you believe in this Mimic thing now?" Brielle said.

"No. Maybe. I don't know." He walked up to the window and glanced outside, at the tower, the finger pushing a purple crown against the cold blue: the devices were already active, an upward pull to hold the giant together. "Listen, Lena and I were on a hunt, right after the duke decommissioned the tulips—"

"The Drakiri devices."

"Right after he'd decommissioned the tulips. We chased a deer across the hillside—you know, the hills to the west of the castle. There was a clearing. The deer vanished."

"What do you mean, vanished?"

"Disappeared. Dropped out of reality. No idea."

"Shea, I'm afraid to ask, but... Were you drunk when that happened?"

"Lena..." Shea swallowed. "Lena saw it, too."

"So she was also of the opinion the deer has *dropped out of reality*?" Brielle raised her hand, palm open, when he glanced at her. "Just trying to assess the facts."

"She said she saw *different colors*."

"Did you try to find out what happened? Maybe a hallucinogen in mushrooms or something, you stepped on them and—"

"She wrote it off as a hallucination too. The deer—we thought it simply ran away from under our noses."

"So..." Brielle took a sip. "I suspect now you've reconsidered."

"Now I've reconsidered."

"May I ask why?"

"Because of this." He took out from his pocket and unfolded the sketch. "There's at least a dozen more of those in, in *her* bedroom. All of the same place where we hunted."

Brielle took the drawing from him and studied it. "She had talent. And this proves what?"

"This *proves* nothing. But maybe, just maybe, there's a possibility..." He looked at the first stars dipped in the water-thin film of clouds. "Maybe a portal of sorts formed there. Is forming. A doorway."

"To the Mimic Tower?"

"Like I said, Brielle, would we be able to tell their superstition from knowledge?"

"Okay. Why are you telling *me* this?"

"Because I need you to go to that place with me."

She chuckled—but, after studying him, her brows came together. "Shea, you've been under a lot of stress lately. You sound... off."

"Perhaps I sound the way I should, for the first time in my life. I need you to go with me because I can't make the decision alone—you were right the other day, I can't shoulder any more blame. I can't betray you, as well. If the decision has to be made, we'll have to make it together."

"Which decision, Shea, what are you—"

"We may need to do something about the tower."

"Like hell we will." She slammed her cup onto the table, and the porcelain swirled in a small pirouette. "You already did something about it, twice—you removed the Drakiri devices, then brought them back. Make up your mind already."

"I—"

"Make up your goddamn mind!"

"I forgive you."

"What?"

"The mistake in the calculations you've made—I forgive you for it."

She frowned. "What the fuck, Shea?"

"I forgive you. It wasn't your fault. The duke's an asshole, he pushed you to the limit, you made a mistake. It's human. It's normal."

Her face twitched.

"I forgive you, do you hear me?" He strode up to her and squeezed her arms. "Do you hear me? I forgive you for your mistake."

Brielle inhaled sharply. "I only wanted to do my job. He'd changed the deadline —"

"It wasn't your fault."

"Others might disagree."

"Then to hell with them. You know? To hell with them."

She kept silent.

"Please. Come with me to the hillside tomorrow, and let's just see what's out there. I owe it to her. If there's even the slightest possibility of her being right, I need to... Otherwise, I won't forgive *me*."

6

The black mane, a cloud of breath embossed by the sunlight. Their horses trudged forward, and the hillside drew nearer, a slope passing from the unformed of the waking world into some semblance of order, into the forest's ragged outlines.

"Do you remember where that place of yours was?" Brielle said.

"A clearing. It was a clearing up the hill."

She snorted. "This is as generic a description as it goes."

"We followed this road." Shea waved at the wide trail between the trees. "Then, at some point, turned off."

"Where exactly?"

"Listen, it was a hunt."

Brielle mumbled something.

"Sorry—didn't hear you."

"I said, what the hell am I even doing here."

Shea didn't answer. He remembered *her*, standing in the stirrups, the smile, the laughter. *Guide me*, he thought. *Allow me to do at least some good.*

But nothing came back—the trail remained just a trail—until, on an impulse, he urged his horse into a gallop, mirroring his speed on that day.

They'd kissed.

They'd made love.

She'd been the smell of bonfire and the taste of strawberries.

"Hey, where do you think you're going?" Brielle called out.

Faster! In Shea's mind, Lena drove her heels into her horse's flanks, and he did the same. A hundred feet more, straight. Left, into the aspen grove, into the thinner path, between the two birches.

The trees ahead parted, and the tower stared at him through the morning haze, the memory and the present twin beads on an invisible umbilical cord.

"That's it. That's it!"

They darted into a clearing. He pulled on the reins and glanced around.

"Are we there? You sure?" Brielle said from behind.

He took out the sketch and held it out to her.

"Well." She shrugged. "Seems similar enough—but then again, it's just trees and a glade."

"Trust me, this is the place. It all happened when we dashed in here."

"I personally didn't experience any visions."

"We came through there, same as now." He pointed at the road behind them.

"Maybe..." she said. "And mind you, don't take this to mean I believe in a doorway to the other dimension or some such. But maybe you and I didn't pass through the right spot? After all, you said yourself the deer disappeared and neither you nor Lena did."

Even more painful to hear another say her name than to say it myself.

He shook his head to disperse the memories. "Worth a shot. Would you please hold my horse for me?"

The path led back into the forest, into the bush where the morning quiet held its sway, only the leaves moving, fawning over the wind. He stretched out his hand and walked toward the trees, waving his palm left and right like a blind man.

The first step, second, third—and then he had no fingers anymore.

An instinct yanked his elbow back.

Somewhere, a branch snapped and a small animal darted into the bushes.

Shit shit shit, his heart drummed out.

"Brielle!"

"What?"

"I think I've found it."

Slowly, he raised his arm again.

Void ate everything up to his wrist, and this time, he made an effort not to recoil. He moved his hand to the left, and the cutoff line across his skin bent: whatever was in front of him seemed to be spherical or cylindrical in shape. He circled the thing in the tiny steps of someone walking along a cliff's edge.

The doorway was probably wide enough to devour a horse, but not wider. One could easily miss it.

"Wait," Brielle said. "Wait, I'm coming."

But he had already taken a step forward, and forward-backward-to-the-side.

Direction didn't matter anymore, and—

The sky bled crimson and orange.

The air that wrapped around him tasted of salt and reeked of rotten eggs.

Something that *resembled* trees— multi-necked, multi-fingered foliage in *vertical* stripes, like someone had stripped the real tree trunks clean and glued brushes to them—pushed the clouds away from the ground's uniform burnt crust.

A bout of wind slapped him in the face, making him turn, and that was when he saw it.

Less of a tower, more of a giant centipede, standing upright and sprouting thorns instead of legs—if thorns could be the size of a house. Behind, a cloud formation—a tornado?—turned around lazily.

He backed away like a sleepwalker.

"What   the…"   Brielle   appeared, breathing in a marathon runner tempo. "What the… Where are we?"

"I don't know," his lips answered.

"This is a hallucination. I'm dreaming, I'm dreaming, dreaming."

You are you are you are, his mind echoed.

"No," he said, "no. We've arrived."

Right there, twenty feet away from him, next to the tree line, lay the decomposing carcass of a deer.

Brielle took a few drunken sailor steps and probed the ground with the tip of her boot. "The soil is baked." She glanced up, and her face changed. "Oh my."

"Exactly."

"I can't believe it."

"The Mimic Tower," he said.

Brielle squinted, raising her hand to the sky, thumb and pinky outstretched, a trembling, but still a professional gesture. "A thousand feet, give or take. Same as ours. Gosh." She opened and closed her mouth. "Am I… Am I responsible for this?"

The   thorns,   like   handles   some inconceivable being might use on its climb to the skies. "Lena said it builds itself— but yes, as far as I understood, it's our tower that allows it… to manifest."

After a brief pause, Brielle chuckled. He glanced at her: *had she gone crazy*?

"Funny how the brain works," she said.

"The brain?"

"I've had a small revelation."

"What do you—"

"Funny." She chuckled again, running her palm through her hair. "If it's all true, then my mistake, Shea—it was actually something good, wasn't it? If she was right. If she was right all along."

She was.

Brielle extended her arm toward him. "There's a freedom in—"

A distant rumble rolled. Her face changed, and he looked where she looked, at the thing he'd taken for clouds.

After all, clouds do resemble people sometimes—*but*, he thought, *while they may look like people, they never move like ones.*

A naked figure, an overgrown baby, shifted against the sky. Only the top part of the body was visible, everything waist-down concealed by the trees so that it looked as though it waded through the forest.

Brielle gasped. "It's a human... a human... a fucking giant."

He felt the hair on his head move. "Not a human."

"Not *entirely* human—"

"The movements, Brielle, look at how it moves."

A fluid half-dance, part walking, part sailing...

"My gosh. Are you saying they're Drakiri—"

"That, or something related." *Heavens, it's huge. Did it see them? Was it able to see in the conventional sense of the word?*

Brielle whispered, "What is this place?"

...only that we'd arrived from elsewhere. The light's orange tint, the vertical foliage—like the drapes in Lena's quarters. Decorating your home in a bow to some vague ancestral memory.

Realization washed over him.

"This is where they came from. Their place of origin. She told me Pangania was a waystation, that they'd come from somewhere else—here."

"Gosh," Brielle said, "my gosh. Maybe a, a catastrophe happened here or—"

At that moment, the air moved. Something ruffled through the brush-like leaves, rising above the trees. The giant's head turned.

It *looked* at Shea—or rather, two stones rolled under the eyelids until the gaze weighed him down. For the longest second in his life, there were only those eyes, black, expressionless—or was it that he didn't *understand* the expression, that it was so vast he simply couldn't wrap his mind around it?

A palm rose from behind the trees, a steady, graceful ascent. Moved forward.

At first, he kept telling himself the giant was too far away to reach them.

Then Brielle screamed, and something crashed into his shoulder: she pushed him out of the way.

"No! Brielle, no!"

But the hand had already closed around her body.

As though on a picture, dashes of white came through: she hammered her fists on the fingers which could've belonged to some colossal monument.

The sight tore Shea free from his paralysis. "Let her go, you mound of shit!" He sprinted, uselessly, after the hand as it moved away at double the speed.

"Destroy it," Brielle screamed when he caught her gaze. "Destroy—"

His foot sank into a hollow in the ground. He lost his balance and fell, stretching out his hands—and as his forearms disappeared, he realized he'd run straight into the other side of the portal.

The next instant, he was back to the forested hillside.

He doubled over and threw up into the morning dew.

"Brielle! Brielle!"

Some sensation returned to his body— all that time, his heart hadn't stopped playing drums on his ribs.

He started, swaying, toward where the doorway was.

The wind changed its tune, and five *things* stretched out of nowhere in front of him—each one could've been a tree trunk. A palm reached into the world and, slowly, swung left to right, feeling for something—or someone, crumpling the bush. Then it retracted back into the portal.

Above, a chickadee sang.

"Brielle! Let her go, you piece of—"

He darted through the spot, but nothing happened—and, frantically, he waved his hands.

This time, his fingers remained his own. He glanced around, at the waking forest, the lazy sunlight. Perhaps the doorway only opened, for each person, only once. *Or perhaps something on the other side didn't want him to come through again.*

The chickadee clung to its bravado.

"Brielle."

He tried for a whole hour, but that was it. The doorway into the world Lena had told him about had closed.

7

Autumn leaves crumbled under his feet.

The horses, finally free, darted past.

Make up your goddamn mind already.

He tore off his jacket and hurled it into the bush. Ice crept under his shirt, but this was okay, this was fine: it was new air, entering his lungs.

Destroy it.

Such a simple idea, really, such a correct one, free from his own former indecisiveness.

Go to hell, Daelyn. I don't want the kingdom, the throne, the golden dance. You can take it all. Take everything. Take my title, my family name, my estate. I don't want any of this. I don't need it.

"You hear me?" he shouted. "Take everything!"

Brielle had been right—there *was* a freedom. In not having a choice anymore.

He descended the hill's slope. The distance clear of the morning's sediment, the tower gained form, its top leaking thick purple into the day.

Thirty-odd Drakiri devices, all in one place. He had to hope an implosion of that magnitude would be enough to bring the mammoth structure down—and with it, if he'd understood everything right, the doorway.

And this time, there would be no changing one's mind, no possibility for a flip-flop, no rosewood trapdoor to go back to.

Forgive me, Lena. I should've listened when you talked. I should've looked. Tulips will finally bloom—for you.

A week after his workshop's destruction, he'd talked to the Drakiri at the town hall, the one who'd warned him. *Five minutes*, the man told him; his sister and Danny had only had five minutes to live from the moment Danny had touched the valve.

Shea didn't know if five minutes would be enough to get out of the implosion radius—or what that radius would be. One tulip had chewed through a two-story building; he could only imagine how far three dozen would reach.

But it hardly mattered anymore.

He expected guards at the entrance; there were only the artisans, diving into the gate's gap-toothed mouth, diving out. The duke had found his saboteurs; Lena was dead; there was no need to waste resources on guards.

He'd found her body over there, in the grass.

Shea reached for his pocket, for her diary—realizing he'd discarded it together with his jacket. He turned around; for a moment, that was all that mattered.

Then he squeezed his fist and entered the tower.

Brielle's beast had beauty. It had perfect symmetry. The spiral staircase folded into a snail's shell above his head, and coals burned, scattered across cities on the steep climb. *Cities*—the impression from his first visit remained like a daguerreotype of a childhood love: settlements built out of pulleys, carts, and treadwheel cranes, shot through with harmonies of tools squeaking in the shadows.

For a moment, the idea of destroying all this—worlds hidden within a world—made the stone weight squeeze around him.

"Hey!" Shea flinched at his own voice ringing through the empty space. "Hey! Everybody leave, now!"

He didn't actually think this would work—but a sprung coil inside demanded release.

Two men approached him, wearing cream-colored aprons and worried faces.

"What's going on?" the taller one said.

"Don't you recognize me?"

The pair exchanged glances. "You're Lord Ashcroft."

"Yes. Lady Brielle asked everyone to vacate the construction site."

"We... we haven't heard anything to that effect."

"The Drakiri devices at the top are about to implode."

Worried faces went chalk-white. "We haven't heard—"

"Do you hear me *now*?" He grabbed the tall guy by the arm. "Hey. Do you? Or shall I spell it out for you louder?"

The man's face was two fears fighting: that of making an administrative mistake and another, a deeper one—for his life.

"What's your name?" Shea said. "All those people die, it's your fault."

That settled it. The artisan turned to his fellow. "Inform the crew. I'll spread the word up."

"No," Shea said. "I'll do it myself. You take care of your own guys. Stay organized, and we'll all get out of this alive."

He headed for the staircase, and through the pain of loss—the one which had happened and the one which was about to happen—euphoria kicked in.

"Vacate the site." He waved at another worker walking past him. "Others are already on their way out."

"Vacate the site."

Heavens, how easy. How laughably easy it was, bending the giant to his will. Same instructions, to anyone he encountered. Soon, it wasn't even needed: on the staircase's second whirl, he counted three men rising in wooden cages, probably to warn the workers at the upper levels, and in ten minutes he had to keep to the wall in order not to be pushed over the edge by the steady stream of people rushing downward.

A domino effect—you see others below, fleeing, your instincts kick in.

By the time he got to the top, he was walking through abandoned towns: a frozen pulley, an overturned bucket, somebody's shirt over a grinding wheel.

The top, however, was still alive, and it was a whole new world.

8

A massive flat platform, sanded to perfect white under the autumn sun, supported the tower's jawline.

He finally understood why his sister had called them 'tulips'. Those bumps in the unfinished wall weren't Drakiri devices—or 'egg-shaped things'—those were flowers, grown through the stone, ready to bloom. Those were gardeners, standing knee-deep in the purple rolling across the wooden planks.

Two people, peeking over the edge.

One of them turned and waved. "Lord Ashcroft. What's happening?" He ran—a clumsy half-walk, half-run, a parody of how Drakiri moved. "Why is everybody fleeing? We were told the devices are about to implode—"

"They are," said Shea.

"But they aren't!" The man stretched out his hands, palms cupped. "We've, we've checked every single one. They're operating as—"

"How long have you been working here?" Shea looked him in the eye, and the hands dropped.

"We—"

"You've made a mistake."

"My lord—"

"This isn't a debate. You don't want to take chances with those things."

Paranoia. I don't know about yours— but that's how our race survives, Lena. That's how we've always survived.

"We've checked every one of them." Practically a whisper now.

Shea pointed at the staircase. "Vacate the site."

"And you, my lord?"

"I'll try to prevent the catastrophe."

The man reminded him of the fellow with sad labrador eyes whom he'd forced to operate a device a month ago: same baggy trousers, same frightened gaze. Same willingness to follow orders, regardless of where they led.

When both workers disappeared down the staircase, he allowed himself to breathe.

Was it him, or had the purple thickened? *The tulips, are they opening for the sun?*

He walked up to the device closest to him. 'Here, let me show you,' she'd said and touched the dark surface, lightly as though weaving or playing a harp.

He put his hands on the valve. Took a second's hesitation he could still afford. And unscrewed the valve, all the way.

He thought he heard chickadees, but, of course, at this height it was impossible.

Something hummed through the tower's arteries. Something woke up within the stone, stirred, and squared its shoulders.

"Away from the device, now."

He turned around. *Four minutes forty seconds.*

In calm, measured steps, Aidan ascended the staircase and stepped onto the platform.

"Away from the device, Shea. Damn—I should've known. Any idiot could see you were too weak to handle power."

"The tower needs to be destroyed. I've been to—"

"Put it back. Whatever you just did, undo it."

"I can't. And I won't—not again."

"I should've known," Aidan said, pulling off his glove, "right there, at the beginning, at the capital. When you'd refused to gas that mob. The plebs. I would've done it without batting an eyelid."

He advanced, rolling the 'fingers' of the knotted contraption he had for a hand. "I need this tower."

"No."

Four minutes.

"I should've simply killed you and fulfilled the queen's mandate myself."

He made a wide swing, and Shea caught him by the wrist—immediately realizing how futile an attempt it was. It was like trying to stop a horse at full speed.

The Drakiri hand must've weighed at least three pounds, and Aidan knew how to use it. All Shea was able to do was deflect it an inch; for a few seconds, he felt his head existing separate from his body, a torn-off part of a rag doll. Next came the pain and the wall's stones, crashing into his forehead.

He slipped and steadied himself. "Fulfilled her mandate?" He spat blood at the white boards. "The duke would've disposed of you, same as he tried with me."

Aidan smiled. "I'm afraid the good old duke is unwell at the moment. Something in the food, I hear. He won't be bothering me any longer."

Three minutes.

Another swing—this time, Shea ducked, and Aidan's fist sent a cloud of crushed rock into the air.

"Think about your country!"

"You're blind in one eye because of your Duma hatred." Shea stabbed his finger at his own bloodied face. "Get it through your head: they aren't attacking is."

"And we won't be waiting for that, either." Aidan spun his arm as though preparing to shoot a sling. "From here, we'll stage a preemptive strike. We'll attack ourselves."

"You're fucking insane."

"Put it back, you idiot!"

"I won't."

Two minutes.

The blow landed on Shea's left biceps, pain spreading through the body like fire: a bone had broken inside.

A spasm made him double over, and at that moment a wave of heat licked his face. He froze. The tulip he'd rigged was opening; it swelled—as though it were a wart the wall tried to push out—and tore itself apart in the process. The heat came from the expanding crease, and he remembered the skin of his fingers melting against the surface of another device, in a different life.

He shifted his gaze to Aidan.

"Time's up," his adversary said, raising his fist. "You're walking away from something I should've had."

"I've never needed it, you fucker. You can have it."

This time, he didn't try to block. With his healthy hand, Shea grabbed Aidan's wrist and deflected the motion right into the purple crease.

The knuckles went in with a screech. Aidan grunted, trying to free himself, and that was when the tulip changed its song. It seemed bigger, a moment later smaller, alternating between two ends of an invisible compressed path.

The device spat Aidan's hand out. The arm bounced in a wide arc like a wooden toy.

Halfway through, the hand exploded.

With a wail, the wall began to bend, the mist at its base collecting itself into a funnel.

Aidan must've been dead the moment his body touched the platform.

Shea froze, staring at the disfigured lump—dreams, ambitions, and memories, under a film of blood and thin white cloth fluttering in the wind.

For a moment, he considered dragging Aidan to safety. Then he realized he had no more time.

The next tulip opened, pulled into the implosion radius of the first. And the next one: a chain reaction.

The beautiful garden his sister had wished for, coming to life.

Shea dashed toward the staircase, a ripple passing through the boards underneath his feet, and he almost made it—right to the first step, where he felt his body being hauled back.

Not like this. Not like this. Ignoring the white-hot pain in his left arm, he waved his hands like a bird and propelled himself forward.

Even in free fall, as the darkness sped up past him, he sensed the tremor which shook the mammoth structure: the collapse had begun.

I did it, Lena. I did it.

And, to his surprise, the abyss answered. *Come home*, it said.

The abyss responded in Lena's voice—only he didn't know which of the two anymore.

Does it matter? he thought, enjoying the numbness that comes with the air battering the body. He let the voice carry him and remembered the dog he'd seen on his penultimate day at the capital, the poor mongrel who'd tried to get at the lamp post. It staggered him how, back then, he'd failed to recognize that desire—to reach something huge, but utterly useless.

A gust of wind spun him around. A treadwheel, a whirl of the staircase. Purple glow from above, blooming for the last time.

It's a dance, it dawned on him. Not the one he'd wished for—an illusion, all lacquer, all empty hopes—but something real, something that rendered even his mistakes, his earlier indecision, insignificant.

"It's a dance!" he shouted, the wind immediately snatching his words.

And who knows, perhaps the final pas isn't the fall.

Perhaps the real dance takes you through the halls, father and farther away, until you come across a room with flowers where a girl with hands made for weaving or playing a harp, a black wave of hair rolling down her shoulders, would raise her head and smile at you.

Welcome you home.

See Yaroslav Barsukov's story "Tower of Mud and Straw IV: The Tower" online at Metaphorosis.
If you liked it, leave a comment. Authors love that!
Remember to subscribe to our e-mail updates so you'll know when new stories are posted.

Copyright

Title information

Metaphorosis December 2020

ISSN: 2573-136X (online)
ISBN: 978-1-64076-183-4 (e-book)
ISBN: 978-1-64076-184-1 (paperback)

Copyright

Copyright ©2020, Metaphorosis Publishing.
Cover art © 2020 by Chris Panatier.
www.chrispanatier.com, @chrisjpanatier

"The Skin of Aquila Cadens" © 2020, Chris Panatier
"The Three Thousand" © 2020, Elise Kim
"Heritage" © 2020, Andrei Pechalin
"Tower of Mud and Straw IV: The Tower" © 2020,
    Yaroslav Barsukov

Authors also retain copyrights to all other material in the
anthology.

Works of fiction

This book contains works of fiction. Characters, dialogue, places, organizations, incidents, and events portrayed in the works are fictional and are products of the author's imagination or used fictitiously. Any resemblance to actual persons, places, organizations, or events is coincidental.

All rights reserved

All rights reserved. With the exception of brief quotations embedded in critical reviews, no part of this publication may be reproduced, distributed, stored, or transmitted in any form or by any means – including all electronic and mechanical means – without written permission from the publisher.

The authors and artists worked hard to create this work for your enjoyment. Please respect their work and their rights by using only authorized copies. If you would like to share this material with others, please buy them a copy.

Moral rights asserted

Each author whose work is included in this book has asserted their moral rights, including the right to be identified as the author of their respective work(s).

Publisher

Metaphorosis
a magazine of speculative fiction

Metaphorosis Magazine is an imprint of Metaphorosis Publishing
Neskowin, OR, USA

www.metaphorosis.com

"Metaphorosis" is a registered trademark.

Discounts available

Substantial discounts are available for educational institutions, including writing workshops. Discounts are also available for quantity purchases. For details, contact Metaphorosis at metaphorosis.com/about

Metaphorosis Publishing

Metaphorosis offers beautifully written science fiction and fantasy. Our imprints include:

Metaphorosis Magazine
Plant Based Press
Verdage

You can also find us:
@MetaphorosisMag, @MetaphorosisRev,
@Metaphorosis
www.facebook.com/metaphorosis

Help keep Metaphorosis running by supporting us at
Patreon.com/metaphorosis

See more about some of our books on the following pages.

Metaphorosis

a magazine of speculative fiction

Metaphorosis is an online speculative fiction magazine dedicated to quality writing. We publish an original story every week, along with author bios, interviews, and notes on story origins.

We also publish monthly print and e-book issues, as well as yearly Best of and Complete anthologies.

Come and see us online at magazine.Metaphorosis.com

Metaphorosis: Best of 2019

The best science fiction and fantasy stories from *Metaphorosis* magazine's fourth year.

Metaphorosis 2019

All the stories from *Metaphorosis* magazine's fourth year. Fifty-two great SFF stories.

Metaphorosis: Best of 2018

The best science fiction and fantasy stories from *Metaphorosis* magazine's third year.

Metaphorosis 2018

All the stories from *Metaphorosis* magazine's third year. Fifty-two great SFF stories.

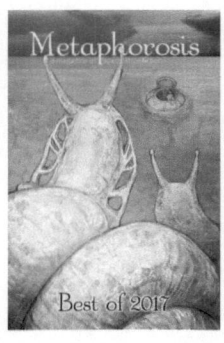 

Metaphorosis: Best of 2017

The best science fiction and fantasy stories from *Metaphorosis* magazine's *second* year.

Metaphorosis 2017

All the stories from *Metaphorosis* magazine's second year. Fifty-three great SFF stories.

Metaphorosis: Best of 2016

Metaphorosis 2016

The best science fiction and fantasy stories from *Metaphorosis* magazine's first year.

Almost all the stories from *Metaphorosis* magazine's first year.

Plant Based Press

plant
based
press

Vegan-friendly science fiction and fantasy, including an annual anthology of the year's best SFF stories.

Best Vegan SFF of 2019

The best vegan-friendly science fiction and fantasy stories of 2019!

Best Vegan SFF of 2018

The best vegan-friendly science fiction and fantasy stories of 2018!

Best Vegan SFF of 2017

The best vegan-friendly science fiction and fantasy stories of 2017!

Best Vegan SFF of 2016

The best vegan-friendly science fiction and fantasy stories of 2016!

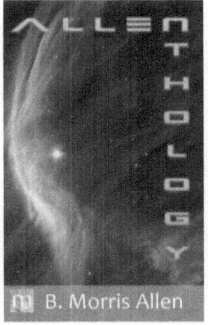

Susurrus

A darkly romantic story of magic, love, and suffering.

Allenthology: Volume I

A quarter century of SFF, including the full contents of the collections *Tocsin, Start with Stones,* and *Metaphorosis*.

Verdage

Science fiction and fantasy books for writers – full of great stories, often with an additional focus on the craft of speculative fiction writing.

Reading 5X5 x2

Duets

How do authors' voices change when they collaborate?

A round-robin of five talented science fiction and fantasy authors collaborating with each other and writing solo.

Including stories by Evan Marcroft, David Gallay, J. Tynan Burke, L'Erin Ogle, and Douglas Anstruther.

Score

an SFF symphony

What if stories were
written like music?
Score is an anthology
of varied stories
arranged to follow an
emotional score from
the heights of joy to
the depths of despair
– but always with a
little hope shining
through.

Reading 5X5

Five stories, five times

Twenty-five SFF authors, five base stories, five versions of each – see how different writers take on the same material.

Reading 5X5

Writers' Edition

Two extra stories, the story seed, and authors' notes on writing. Over 100 pages of additional material specifically aimed at writers.

www.ingramcontent.com/pod-product-compliance
Lightning Source LLC
Chambersburg PA
CBHW030205130726
47898CB00012B/880